NORAH McCLINTOCK

CLOSE TO THE HEEL

PAPL
DISCARDED

ORCA BOOK PUBLISHERS

Library and Archives Canada Cataloguing in Publication

McClintock, Norah
Close to the heel / Norah McClintock.
(Seven (the series))

Issued also in an electronic format.
ISBN 978-1-55469-950-6

I. Title. II. Series: Seven the series
PS8575.C62C56 2012   jC813'.54   C2012-902623-9

First published in the United States, 2012
Library of Congress Control Number: 2012938309

Summary: At the request of his late grandfather, Rennie goes to Iceland
to right an old wrong, and gets drawn into investigating a murder.

*Orca Book Publishers is dedicated to preserving the environment and has
printed this book on Forest Stewardship Council® certified paper.*

Orca Book Publishers gratefully acknowledges the support for its publishing
programs provided by the following agencies: the Government of Canada
through the Canada Book Fund and the Canada Council for the Arts,
and the Province of British Columbia through the BC Arts Council
and the Book Publishing Tax Credit.

Design by Teresa Bubela
Cover photography by Getty Images

ORCA BOOK PUBLISHERS
PO Box 5626, Stn. B
Victoria, BC Canada
V8R 6S4

ORCA BOOK PUBLISHERS
PO Box 468
Custer, WA USA
98240-0468

www.orcabook.com
Printed and bound in Canada.

15 14 13 12 • 5 4 3 2

To Jens with thanks for a new waterfall
(or two, or three) and a new folktale every day.

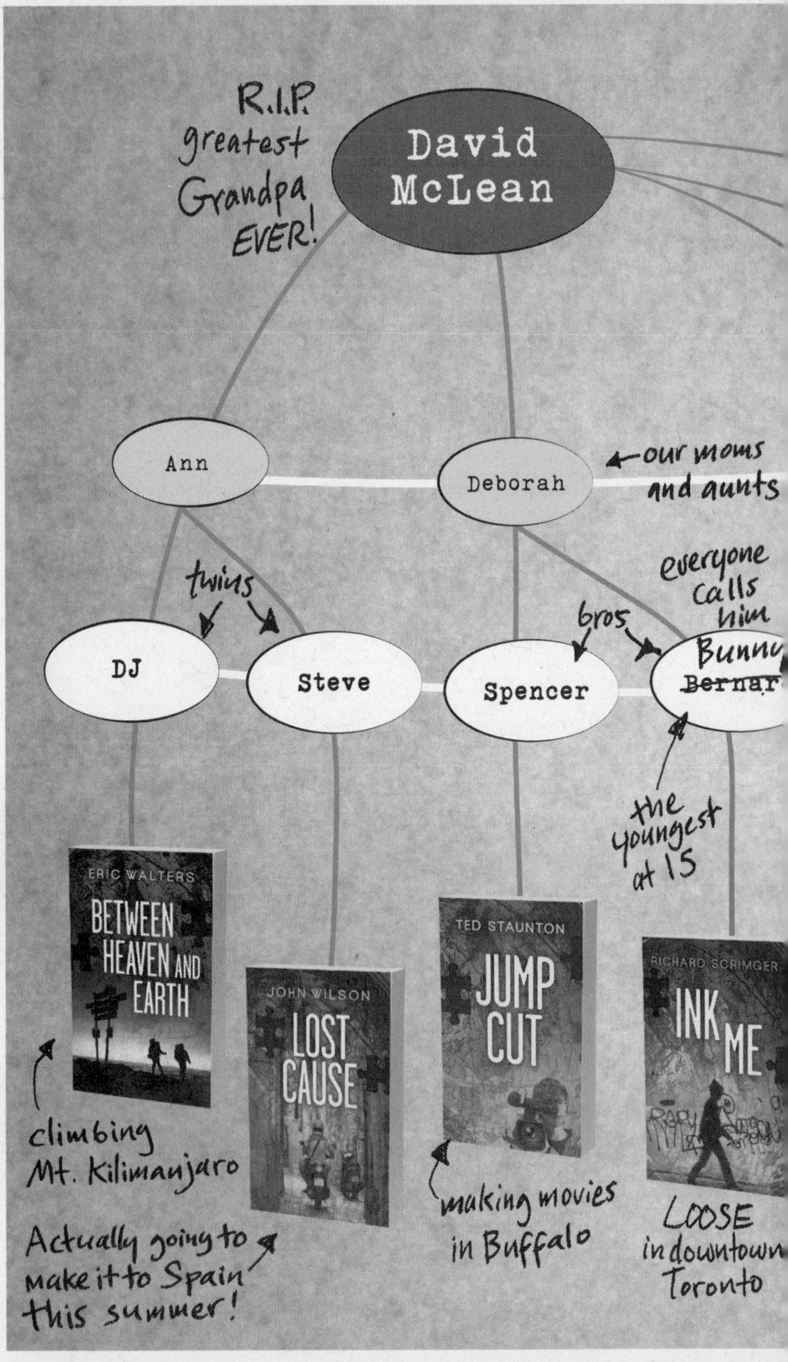

R.I.P. greatest Grandpa EVER!
David McLean
Ann
Deborah
our moms and aunts
twins
DJ
Steve
bros
Spencer
everyone calls him Bunny
Bernar
the youngest at 15
ERIC WALTERS
BETWEEN HEAVEN AND EARTH
JOHN WILSON
LOST CAUSE
TED STAUNTON
JUMP CUT
RICHARD SCRIMGER
INK ME
climbing Mt. Kilimanjaro
Actually going to make it to Spain this summer!
making movies in Buffalo
LOOSE in downtown Toronto

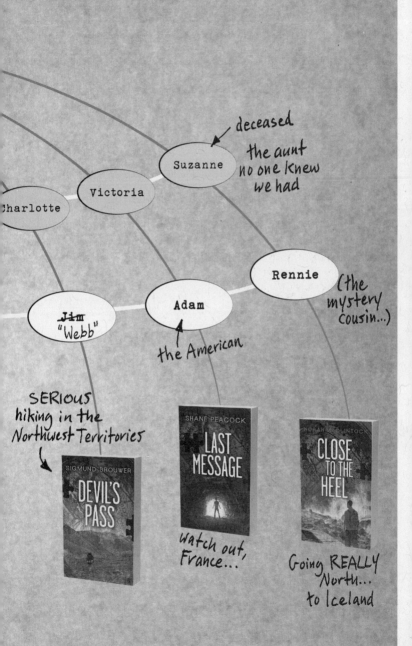

deceased

Suzanne

the aunt
no one knew
we had

Victoria

Charlotte

Rennie

(the
mystery
cousin...)

Adam

Jim
"Webb"

the American

SERIOUS
hiking in the
Northwest Territories

SIGMUND BROUWER

DEVIL'S
PASS

SHANE PEACOCK

LAST
MESSAGE

Watch out,
France...

NORAH McCLINTOCK

CLOSE
TO THE
HEEL

Going REALLY
North...
to Iceland

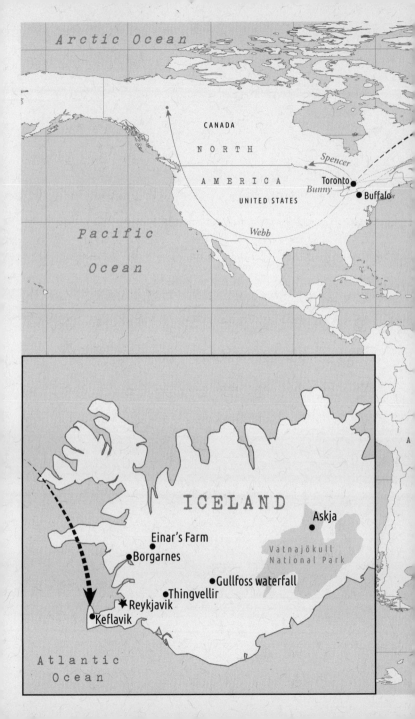

Arctic Ocean

CANADA

NORTH

AMERICA

UNITED STATES

Spencer

Toronto

Bunny

Buffalo

Pacific

Ocean

Webb

ICELAND

Askja

Vatnajökull
National Park

Einar's Farm

Borgarnes

Gullfoss waterfall

Thingvellir

Reykjavik

Keflavik

Atlantic

Ocean

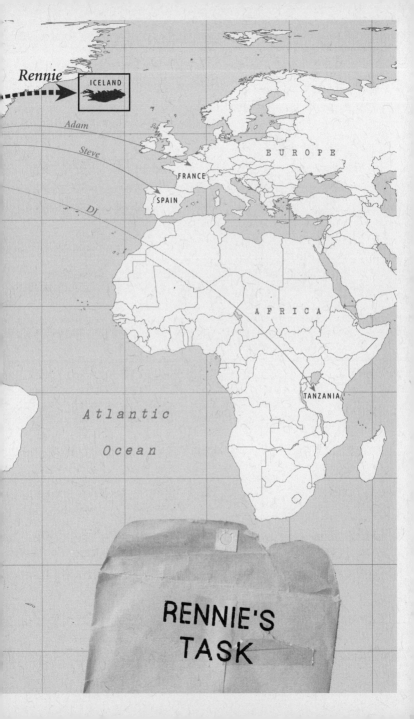

The door hath swung too near the heel;
But better sore feet than serve the Deil.

—FROM "THE BLACK SCHOOL"
AN ICELANDIC FOLKTALE

ONE

I'm going to die. It's as simple as that.

The thought makes my heart feel hollow, but what can I do?

I drag one foot up out of the snow. Snow! It's only October. I will it to move forward and feel it sink again into the whiteness. I pray that it will find solid ground and not a bottomless crevice.

My foot touches down on something hard. I know that not because I feel it land—I don't— but because I'm lifting my left leg, which I could only do if my right foot were firmly planted. I force myself to plod on.

I have no idea where I am, except that it's somewhere in the interior. At least, I think it is.

I have no idea how long I've been here.

I have no idea what direction I'm going in or what direction I should be going in.

I have no idea how far I've gone or how far I need to go.

The only thing I'm sure of is that I'm not going to make it.

I know my feet are down there at the ends of my legs, but I can't feel them. I can't see them either. I can't see anything except white, and I don't know if the white I see is snow or snow blindness. My eyes are burning. They're also watering, and that makes me afraid they will freeze solid in my head. I've stopped shivering, but I can't decide if that's good or bad. At first when the shivering stopped, I ached all over. I know what that's from—muscle fatigue from so much violent trembling or pain from the cold. Either way, it scares me because all I can think of is the amount of energy I'm expending. It takes a while before I realize I'm not cold anymore. Maybe the snow is insulating me. Or maybe—this is the part I don't want to think about—maybe you stop shivering when your body temperature falls below a certain point.

I'm going to die.

So why don't I surrender? Why don't I stop slogging through snow that's up to my knees, making each step feel like the equivalent of ten? Why don't I sit down and just let it happen? Or, even better, lie down and give in to it? The snow is soft. It's thick too. If I lie on it, it will feel like a feather mattress or at least like what I imagine a feather mattress would feel like. I could stretch out and relax myself into the next world, assuming there is a next world. It wouldn't hurt. That's what they say anyway. They say when you freeze to death, you just lie down and go to sleep, and the next thing you know (except you don't really know, because how can you?), you're gone. You've slipped away. Passed over. Ventured to the land from which no one has ever returned. What Shakespeare called the undiscovered territory. (Thank you, Mr. Banks; you always said that knowledge of Shakespeare provides a person with a wealth of images to draw on later in life.)

I drag my foot up again and coax it to take another step. Come on, leg. Don't fail me now.

Don't let it end this way, in the middle of nowhere where I'll never be found.

I think that's what keeps me moving—the thought of never being found. That and the fact that I've never been known to back down, let alone surrender.

And the fact that the one thing I *do* know is *why* I'm here.

I take another step.

I think about the Major and everything he's tried to pound into my head for the last seventeen years. If there's one thing the Major hates, it's a quitter. He says no one was born composing symphonies (except maybe Mozart). Everyone has to start somewhere. You have to walk before you can run. Every journey starts with the first step.

And continues with the next and then the next.

You have to stick to it. They didn't put a man on the moon by giving up after the first rocket fizzled. Wars aren't won by armies who are prepared to surrender after the first defeat.

I pick up my foot again. I still can't feel it, by which I mean I can't tell if I'm actually wiggling my toes or if I just think I'm wiggling toes that are way past being able to wiggle no matter what orders the brain sends down the line. But I do know that someone must have tied a couple of cement bricks to each of my ankles, because I can barely lift my feet. After a couple more steps, I sink to my knees. I'm done. My goose is baked, as the Major would say. I can think of another way to put it, but the Major has this thing about four-letter words. He says anyone who uses them is displaying the pathetic state of his vocabulary. If he hears one, he sends me to the dictionary to find five alternatives. If he were a drill sergeant, the army would be a whole different place.

The wind sweeps snow over me as I try to breathe rhythmically, a trick I was taught to keep me calm. It's not long before I'm up to my thighs in snow, and it's funny how it makes me feel warm.

I crouch down until I'm sitting on my heels. I tell myself that it's just for a few minutes, that all I need to do is catch my breath. It feels good to be resting. It feels so good.

My head jerks up, and I realize I've been asleep.

I panic.

I try to scramble to my feet and end up facedown in the snow instead.

I panic again. It's something I'm getting good at.

I push myself up to a squatting position, which sounds like it should be easy to do but isn't. From there I try to stand up. I fall again. Blackness envelopes me— the blackness of terror. I really am going to die. If I don't get up and get moving, it really will be over.

Another thing the Major likes to say: You can't win if you don't play.

You can't get anywhere if you don't take at least one step, Rennie, I tell myself.

I manage to stand. I sway against the wind and the snow. I feel dizzy. I'm going to fall again.

And then something kicks in. It's not a survival instinct, not really. No, instead it's what I've been told is my worst quality and my principal character defect: the need to get even. I may not know where I am or how I got here or, more importantly, how I'm going to get out of here. But I remind myself that I do know *why* I'm here.

I take a step.

I know why I'm here and I know what I'm supposed to do here. I'm *supposed* to disappear. I'm supposed to vanish without a trace, leaving anyone who knows me to shake their head and say,

"He did it again. Rennie's been a screwup ever since, well, ever since forever, so it's no surprise that he screwed up again. What do you expect from a kid like that?"

Except that that's not what happened.

I didn't screw up this time. No, for once it was someone else. Someone who wants me out of the way.

I take another step. It isn't any easier, but I don't even think about stopping or resting. Another Major-ism: You can rest when you're dead.

I'm not taking the fall for this. I am not going gentle into this miserable night (another nod to Mr. Banks and his second idol, Dylan Thomas). Not me. Not Rennie Charbonneau.

No, I want to get even.

I want revenge.

TWO

One thing I know about myself, thanks to a summer of wilderness "fun" (read: forcible confinement in a privately run boot camp for screwups like me) is that I'm fueled by rage. A "counselor" actually said that to me. We, meaning me, Jimi (real first name), Boot (real last name), Capone (real first name—I am *not* kidding) and Worm (first syllable of real last name that, if you ask me, truly captures the essence of the guy), were sitting around the old Coleman stove with the counselor, Gerard—not Gerry—a wannabe shrink who was working at the camp to pay off student loans before heading back to school.

We were supposedly on a canoe trip, but so far we had carried the stupid things more than we had paddled them. In fact, we had spent most of the day on an uphill portage, with the promise—in a couple of days' time—of the most "spectacular" stretch of river we had ever seen.

Jimi, Boot, Capone, Gerard and I were all about the same height, give or take. Worm, on the other hand, was a good head and a half shorter than me. Guess who I got paired with?

So there we were, climbing uphill pretty much all day, which is tough enough with a canoe on your head, and tougher still when it decides to rain— all day. It's even worse when a certain vertically challenged Worm is your partner. We tried it with him in front. My thinking was that since he was uphill and I was downhill, our height difference would more or less cancel itself out. But it turned out that Worm had trouble sticking to the trail. He kept veering off in one direction or another, claiming to be looking for the best footing. I can just imagine what he would have been like in a car. He'd be zooming down the sidewalk or swerving onto people's lawns, convinced that they were faster than the road.

After an hour of that, *I* decided to take the lead. But you try being the tall guy going uphill with a canoe on *your* head. It felt like all the weight was on me. Plus, Worm complained the whole time that he was doing all the work until I was ready to strangle him or, more constructively, switch it up and let him take the lead again. Which meant going off the trail again. Finally I couldn't stand it anymore.

I set down the front of the canoe and let him stagger dangerously close to a patch of poison ivy. It would serve him right if he stepped in it. When he whined at me to help him, I told him to help himself because I was through. He dropped the canoe, putting a great big dent into one side of it, which was going to make it a bear to paddle when—or should I say, if—we ever saw water again. We were so far behind everyone else that no one even noticed. I told him what a loser he was. I gave him a hard time for being short (not his fault, I know), stupid (probably not his fault) and irritating (definitely his fault). Result: he took a swing at me. Not a good idea. Not only am I taller, but I am also smarter *and* I know a thing or three about combat.

When we finally reached the top of the hill we had been climbing—all day—Gerard and the other three guys were like cartoon characters come to life. First, they all gave themselves whiplash from the double take they did, in almost perfect unison. Second, their eyes all *sproinged* out of their heads. Then third, they all started to laugh, even Gerard, although he caught himself pretty fast and switched to a stern look. I guess I can't blame him, because there was Worm with a sleeping bag duct-taped to his head to make him more or less the same height as me, his hands duct-taped to the cross-bars of the canoe so he wouldn't be tempted to put it down again and duct tape over his mouth so he couldn't complain.

Anyway, it was that night, while we were putting up our tents and getting ready to cook our chow, that Gerard said, "Rennie, if they could fuel cars with what you're fueled with, we wouldn't have an energy crisis." Turns out he wasn't supposed to share that kind of opinion with me. Turns out he's supposed to leave the analysis to the real shrinks who swanned into camp once every two weeks to update their assessments of the "funsters" (read: inmates).

The way they—the shrinks—talked about it, being fueled by rage was a bad thing. But, if you ask me (and they did), the most important stuff I ever accomplished happened when I was good and angry. Like when Mr. Dickhead—er, Dick*son*—my grade-nine math teacher, picked on me every day, making me go up to the board and do math problems even though he knew I would get them wrong. One day—there's always that one day—I'd had enough. The whole class had had enough. No one thought it was funny anymore except, I guess, Mr. Dickhead. I decided to get even.

I grabbed Randall Schtirr that Friday after school, made him an offer he couldn't refuse and holed up with him all weekend. When Monday morning math class rolled around, I slumped at my desk, as usual. I got called on, as usual. I slouched my way to the chalkboard, as usual. Mr. Dickhead stood there, back to me, arms crossed over his chest, smug expression on his face (also as usual, although I didn't know that until later) until he heard me put down the chalk. He turned. He looked at the chalkboard. The expression on his face was what they call in those credit-card commercials "priceless." I know because

Randall captured the whole thing on his phone. You can check it out on the web if you're interested.

Everyone in the whole class laughed when they saw that look on his face, like he was staring at an equation written by the guy in the movie about the crazy math genius. Then he got mad and—get this— accused me of cheating. Even kids who didn't particularly like me got their backs up at that.

"Go ahead," I said. "Search me." He wasn't going to find any crib notes on me. The whole thing was in my head. For a change, I'd done my homework— with a lot of help from Randall.

He searched me anyway. Made me turn out my pockets right there in front of the class. Made me roll up my sleeves to prove I didn't have anything written on my arms. Made me hitch up my shirt to check my belly. Was ready, I'm sure of it, to make me drop my pants, except that when I bared my stomach, Megan Lindover said, "I don't think you're allowed to do that, sir."

Mr. Dickhead exploded and sent me to the office for "cheating and being a general pain in the a**." Randall trotted behind me, which, I think, confused Mr. Dickhead.

Mr. Ashton, the principal, freaked when he saw the video on Randall's phone. I think he was imagining what the Major would say when he saw it. He put Mr. Dickhead on suspension—paid, of course. Then other kids started to complain to their parents about Mr. Dickhead. The parents went to the principal. Mr. Dickhead got fired. I was, briefly, a hero at school.

So, you see, anger isn't so bad.

Neither is revenge.

It works for me. All I have to do now is get out of here alive.

By now you're probably wondering: How did he get there in the first place? And where, exactly, is *here*?

Last question first. "Here" is Iceland, a small island just east of Greenland. When I say small, I mean 103,000 square kilometers—or about the size of the state of Kentucky. A grand total of 313,000 people live here, most of whom (200,000) live in or around the capital, Reykjavik, which is in the extreme southwest of the island. Everyone else is scattered around the edges of the island on farms or in tiny villages.

It's the kind of place where, in the winter, it's dark all day except for maybe three hours. No wonder people here have all these crazy stories about trolls and invisible people living in rocks—and believe me, there's a lot of rock in Iceland, thanks to all the volcanoes, which have a habit of erupting and causing widespread devastation, not to mention vast lava fields. Yeah, it's quite the place.

So what am I doing here?

It all started ten days ago—exactly three weeks after I got back from my summer in Northern Ontario, a fun time away from my current fun home at Canadian Forces Base Borden.

THREE

Part of me wanted to run faster, but it was just a small part. The rest of me wanted not to run at all. I mean, why rush into the arms of grief if you don't have to, especially if the person on grief-distribution duty is a certain Major André Charbonneau, ex-soldier, ex-cop, currently employed by the Canadian Forces National Investigation Service, the armed forces equivalent of a major crimes unit of a large police force. One tough guy—that's my dad, the Major.

And what had I done to deserve grief, you might ask? My current crime was tardiness. Yeah, you heard it right. I was running a little late, which, for anyone in the armed forces, is a *major crime*. Unless I missed my guess—and I hardly ever do when it comes to my dad—the Major was standing at attention on the front walk of the crappy little house we'd been assigned for this posting, his head swiveling from side to side like he was watching a tennis match, scanning the environs for Yours Truly while steam blew out of his ears.

The first words out of his mouth, when he finally saw me, would be: "You see that thing on your wrist? That's a watch."

At least, that's what he'd start to say. But the Major is excellent at his job. When lesser CFNIS members talk shop over brewskis at the end of the day, they talk about the legendary Major Charbonneau. He never misses a thing. Also, he's used to giving orders. Used to having them obeyed. Used to interrogating people. Used to getting answers. Used to winning.

The Major would notice right away that my watch, the one he gave me when I turned thirteen, the one that was supposed to guarantee that I was never late, wasn't on my wrist. He'd switch his priorities from chewing me out for being late to demanding, "Where's your watch, mister?" He called me mister whenever he was revving himself up on the pissed-off-o-meter. He only used my real name, which he insisted on pronouncing as if it were French—René, instead of Rennie—when he was in a good mood. For the Major, that meant when he wasn't preoccupied, overworked, exhausted, impatient, annoyed, or any combination thereof. In other words, hardly ever. My name, like everything else between my mom and the Major, was a compromise. The Major's dad's name had been René. Mom said no one would ever pronounce it right in Alberta, where the Major was stationed at the time, so why not make life easier on me? According to the Major, on those rare—as in, once-in-a-blue-moon—occasions when he was feeling mellow, my mom was the only non-military person on the planet who consistently got her way with him. She must have used up the Major's entire compromise quota, because I had never won an argument with him in my life. Not that I didn't try.

I didn't turn on the speed, because the faster I ran, the sooner the Major would get fixated on my bare wrist—bare, that is, except for the rattlesnake tattoo that he hated—and the sooner he'd third-degree me until I'd finally have to tell him (just to get him off my back) that I'd traded my watch to a guy for a first-generation iPod. I could save him a lot of misery by telling him right away what I'd done. But—you probably don't know this—jazzing an army cop when you're not in the army can be a lot of fun. At least, it can if you're me.

I hadn't set out to be late, although I'm sure the shrink I used to see would have disagreed. He would have said that, subconsciously, I was going for that edgy thrill you get when you purposely fly up the nose of a guy who's twice as strong as you are and has a short fuse. The Major would have said that, subconsciously, I was late because I *loved* to piss him off. But that wasn't true. There was nothing subconscious about it.

Surprise number one: the Major wasn't standing on the front walk when I finally rounded the corner onto our street.

Surprise number two: he didn't start hollering at me the moment I came through the front door.

Surprise number three: he wasn't alone. There was some old guy with him. He had gray hair and a neatly trimmed gray beard, and he was wearing a dark suit. He smiled when he saw me.

"You must be Rennie," he said, thrusting out a hand.

"The *late* Rennie." The Major scowled disapprovingly at me. His eyes went to my wrist—See what I mean?—and his scowl deepened. "I told you four o'clock, mister."

I mumbled an insincere-sounding sorry and turned to look at the old guy.

"I'm John Devine," he said. "I was your grandfather's lawyer."

I was pretty sure he wasn't talking about the grandfather I'd sort-of been named after. He had died right before I was born. He had to mean the other one, the one I only found out about after my mom died.

"*Was* his lawyer?" I said.

"He passed away. I'm sorry."

"When?"

"A little over two months ago."

"Two *months* ago?" I turned furiously to the Major.

"I didn't know, Rennie," he said. "The first I heard of it was fifteen minutes ago when Mr. Devine arrived."

I believed him. One thing the Major never did was lie, not even to me.

"Perhaps we can all sit down," Mr. Devine said.

We went into the living room. Mr. Devine sat on the couch. I sat on an armchair. The Major grabbed the remote from the top of the TV and took another armchair.

"What happened?" I asked. "How did he die?"

"Natural causes," Mr. Devine said. "At his age, things just give out." I guessed that was true. The old guy had been pretty slow by the time I'd met him.

Mr. Devine set his briefcase in his lap and clicked open the hasps. He took out an envelope, closed the case again and put the envelope facedown on the coffee table. "I'll answer all of your questions in due course," he said. "Major, if you wouldn't mind, perhaps we could watch that DVD now."

The Major held out the remote and pressed one button to turn on the TV and another to start the DVD. Suddenly, there was my grandfather on the screen, looking pretty much the same as he had the last—and first—time I'd seen him.

"I'm not sure why I have to be wearing makeup," he said, turning to face somebody off camera. "This is my will, not some late-night talk show... and it's certainly not a *live* taping."

A couple of people laughed offscreen. My grandfather turned to the camera.

"Good morning…or afternoon, boys," he began.

Boys? Who was he talking to?

"If you're watching this, I must be dead, although on this fine afternoon I feel very much alive."

I peered at the face on the screen. It was impossible to tell when he'd made the recording. For all I knew, it could have been a year ago or even longer. Or—I swallowed hard—it could have been just before I met him back in early spring. Or just after. Had he known then that he wouldn't be around now? Had he been sick, had things been giving out, and I'd been too stupid or too self-absorbed to notice?

"I want to start off by saying that I don't want you to be too sad," he said, as if he was right there in front of me, reading my mind the way he'd seemed to during my unexpected stay with him. "I had a good life and I wouldn't change a minute of it. That said, I still hope that you are at least a little sad and that you miss having me around. After all, I was one *spectacular* grandpa!"

He wasn't kidding! Five minutes after I'd met him, I'd found myself wishing I'd known him my whole life.

"And you were simply the best grandsons a man could ever have."

Oh, he was talking to my cousins. And to me, I guess, which was why Mr. Devine was here.

Maybe the others had been fantastic grandsons—I didn't know them, so I couldn't say. If he was including me, it wasn't because of anything I had done. It was because that's the kind of guy he was. At least, it was the kind of guy he had seemed like to me, a guy who treats a garbageman the same way he'd treat Bill Gates—with warmth and dignity.

"I want you to know that of all the joys in my life, you were among my greatest. From the first time I met each of you to the last moments I spent with you—and of course I don't know what those last moments were, but I know they were wonderful—I want to thank you all for being part of my life. A very big, special, wonderful, warm part of my life."

Okay, *that* didn't refer to me.

His hand shook as he took a sip from a glass of water.

"I wanted to record this rather than just have my lawyer read it out to you. Hello, Johnnie."

I glanced at Mr. Devine. He was smiling fondly at the image on the screen.

"Johnnie, I hope you appreciate that twenty-year-old bottle of Scotch I left you," he said. "And you better not have had more than one snort of it before the reading of my will! But knowing you the way I do, I suspect you would have had two."

Mr. Devine chuckled.

"I just wanted—needed—to say goodbye to all of you in person, or at least as in person as this allows." His hand was still shaking as he took another sip from his glass.

"Life is an interesting journey, one that seldom takes you where you think you might be going. Certainly I never expected that I was going to become an old man. In fact, there were more than a few times when I was a boy that I didn't believe I was going to live to see another day, never mind live long enough to grow old."

I knew what he meant. He'd told me a lot about his life. He'd been a pilot during World War II and traveled a lot after that. He'd been in more than a few scrapes, and the way he'd described them, most of them had been more serious than any mess I'd ever been in.

"But I did live a long and wonderful life. I was blessed to meet the love of my life, your grandmother Vera. It's so sad that she passed on before any of you had a chance to meet her."

He didn't mean *my* grandmother. He meant the woman he'd actually been married to. That was okay too. He'd been pretty upfront with me about her. He'd told me how much he'd loved her. He'd met my grandmother after his wife died, and he'd loved her too. But she didn't want to get married, not then anyway, and she'd never told him that she was already pregnant when she left him. He didn't know about my mom at all until he read about her death in the national newspaper and saw my grandma's name. Then he'd done the math.

I zoned out after that because he wasn't talking about my grandma; he was talking about his wife. I didn't tune back in until he said, "You boys, you wonderful, incredible, lovely boys, have been such a blessing…seven blessings. Some blessings come later than others."

Did he mean me? So now my cousins knew about me too. Interesting.

"I've done a lot, but it doesn't seem that time is going to permit me the luxury of doing everything I wished for. So, I have some requests, some *last* requests. In the possession of my lawyer are some envelopes. One for each of you."

I glanced at Mr. Devine. He nodded. There was one for me too.

"Each of these requests, these tasks, has been specifically selected for you to fulfill. All of the things you will need to complete your task will be provided—money, tickets, guides. Everything."

Guides? What would I need a guide for?

"I am not asking any of you to do anything stupid or unnecessarily reckless—certainly nothing as stupid or reckless as I did at your ages. Your parents may be worried, but I have no doubts. Just as I have no doubts that you will all become fine young men. I am sad that I will not be there to watch you all grow into the incredible men I know you will become. But I don't need to be there to know that will happen. I am so certain of that. As certain as I am that I will be there with you as you complete my last requests, as you continue your life journeys."

Grandfather lifted up his glass.

"A final toast. To the best grandsons a man could ever have. I love you all so much. Good luck."

The screen went black.

I felt like I had been encased in concrete. I could see. I could breathe, but just barely. But I couldn't move.

The old man was dead.

He'd died over two months ago, and no one told me.

"Was there a funeral?" I asked.

Mr. Devine nodded.

"And?" I said. Anger and resentment collided inside me, the two emotions that caused me the most trouble. "They didn't want me there, is that it?"

"No, that's not it," Mr. Devine said. "As soon as I got the news, I made every attempt to contact you. But you had moved, and ever since the nine-eleven attacks…" His voice trailed off. He didn't have to explain. I'd been hearing that phrase for practically my whole life. It was as if the whole world had been turned upside down on that one day. Nine-eleven explained a lot of the stupid rules the Major had to follow. It explained the ridiculous level of security on every base I had ever been on. It even explained why I'd been hauled out of line in front of all the other airline passengers once, ordered to remove my shoes and stick my arms out so I could be wanded like some kind of wannabe jihadist. "Let's just say that I had to jump through a few hoops before I could locate you and your father, and by the then it was too late for the funeral. As for my mission at this time— your grandfather specified a meeting in person, and since you were, uh, unavailable…" He paused. He was referring to the wilderness boot camp the Major forced me to go to. "Your grandfather thought highly of you, Rennie."

"He did?" I'd thought highly of him too, once I'd met him. I'd been thinking it would be nice if he felt the same way about me. After all, we'd sure seemed to hit it off. "Really? He said that?"

"He did indeed," Mr. Devine said. "And he directed me to give you this." He picked up the envelope and handed it to me.

I stared at it. I wasn't sure that I wanted to open it in front of the Major.

"You have to read it now, Rennie," Mr. Devine said. "That way, I can answer any questions you might have."

My hand actually shook when I ripped it open. I pulled out a typewritten letter and read it silently.

Dear Rennie,

One of the biggest regrets of my life is that I never knew your mother. That makes me feel all the more fortunate that I was able to get to know you before it was too late.

I know you have been through a lot, blamed yourself for things that are not your fault and punished yourself when no punishment was called for. Believe it or not, you aren't the only person to have done this. There are times in every-one's life when we confuse sorrow with blame, when being powerless makes us lash out in anger and when we do things that we regret. Often this happens when a loved one dies, leaving us to wonder why this had to happen to them, why it didn't happen to us instead.

Now I will tell you another of my regrets.

A long time ago, a plane I was flying had engine trouble. If it hadn't happened in the middle of a blizzard and if

I hadn't been a bit hungover, I might have been able to save the day. But that isn't what happened. The plane crashed in the interior of Iceland. I was the only person who walked away—and then only after my best friend died in my arms.

I was near death when an angel appeared and guided me to a sheltered spot. I have never forgotten her face, as you will see. When she faded from sight, I thought she had abandoned me to the afterlife. But when I opened my eyes again, a young doctor named Sigurdur was standing over me. I believed it was a miracle that he had found me. It was only a few days later that I recalled seeing a red scarf marking the spot where I lay.

When Sigurdur came to visit me in the hospital, he said I had imagined the scarf. He grew uncomfortable at my talk of the angel. And so I let it be. It was only recently, as I went through my belongings, that I found a letter in the pack I carried that day. The letter convinced me that the angel was real. I suspect, but cannot prove, that Sigurdur knew this all along. I do not know why he denied it. The letter also stirred up new regrets.

It is perhaps foolish to dwell on something that happened so long ago. I owe Sigurdur as much as I owe my angel. But he is gone now, and, though I never knew her name, I suspect she is too.

Mr. Devine will give you something. I want you to take it to the interior of Iceland—he will tell you exactly where— and bury it, for my angel and for my friend. I can never make up for that day, but with your help I can acknowledge it and memorialize it.

Sincerely,

Your grandfather, David McLean

When I had finished, both the Major and Mr. Devine were looking at me.

"He says you have something that he wants me to deliver," I said to Mr. Devine.

He nodded, opened his briefcase again and pulled out a small package wrapped in brown paper and tied with string. I opened it and stared at the small journal inside. I flipped it open. Dozens of its browned pages were filled with sketches of a woman—the same woman. There was something else—a sheet of pale-blue paper tightly folded and brittle with age. I unfolded it carefully and scanned the writing, but it was old-fashioned, spidery writing and hard to read.

"What does his letter say?" the Major asked.

"He wants me to do something."

"What?"

31

FOUR

"No," the Major said when I told him, making the decision the way he makes all his decisions, without hesitation.

"Mr. McLean made provision for all expenses to be covered and for a guide to take Rennie on this journey, if that's what you're concerned about," Mr. Devine said. In contrast to the Major, he was almost Zenlike.

"That's not what I'm worried about," the Major said. "He's *not* going."

The old me would have been in his face before he finished talking. The old me would have told him where to get off, right after daring him to try to stop me. But I wasn't the old me anymore. At least, I was trying hard not to be.

Instead, I counted to ten slowly—twice. Only then did I say, in a reasonable tone, "But it's what Grandpa wanted."

"Grandpa!" the Major snorted. "Eight months ago, you didn't know the man, and now you call him Grandpa?"

My cheeks started to burn. My hands started to curl into fists. Those were my warning signs. If I didn't do something right away, my temper would get away from me.

I drew in a deep breath. I forced myself to think of my long-term objective—to get the Major to agree to let me go—and to strategize the best way of achieving that. It sure wouldn't be by yelling and screaming.

"But he *was* my grandfather," I said in a quiet voice.

"I don't care if he was Père Noël," the Major said. "You are not going and that's that."

Mr. Devine gazed evenly at the Major for a moment.

"Mr. McLean made full provision for Rennie's further education," he said.

33

"Further education?" The Major stared at him as if he'd said the old man had made provision for my transport to Mars.

"Rennie indicated to Mr. McLean that he wanted to go to university," Mr. Devine said.

The Major stared at me, waiting for an explanation for this ridiculous statement.

"It's true," I said, bracing myself for what I was sure would follow.

"You don't have the grades, Rennie."

"I know. That's why I enrolled in school again." I didn't mention that it was an alternative school. To the Major, alternative meant phoney.

"You what?" I'd seen a lot of expressions on the Major's face recently, but that particular kind of surprise wasn't one of them.

"I figure if I work my butt off, I can get into Lakehead."

"Lakehead?"

"They have an outdoor recreation and parks program there. I want to take it."

The Major was looking at me now as if he was pretty sure that someone or something alien had taken over my body, or at least my brain.

"What are you going to do with that?" he asked.

"Maybe work in a national or provincial park. I don't know."

The Major let out a long sigh. There it was: *I don't know.* There was no alien. It was all me. *Monsieur Je-ne-sais-pas.* That's what he called me—a lot. What are your plans for tonight, Rennie? I don't know. What the hell do you think you're doing, Rennie? I don't know. Where the hell did you get such a stupid idea, Rennie? I don't know. *Je ne sais pas.*

"You're not going."

"But Grandpa—"

"No."

"Mr. Charbonneau—" Mr. Devine began.

"*Major* Charbonneau."

The lawyer nodded. "Mr. McLean has made similar requests of his other grandsons."

"They're all going to Iceland?"

"Not exactly. One is going to climb Kilimanjaro—"

Why couldn't *that* have been me?

"Another is making his way to Spain."

Spain sounded good too.

"Each boy has a request to fulfill. Their parents have all agreed."

"I don't do things just because other people do them, Mr. Devine," the Major said. That was true enough. "And I don't appreciate anyone, least of all a complete stranger, presuming to tell me what I should and shouldn't allow my son to do."

"I would never make such a presumption," Mr. Devine said. "But…" He sighed and produced another envelope from his inside pocket. This one he handed to the Major, who ripped it open and began to read. His face was ferocious with annoyance when he started but had softened somewhat by the end. He folded the letter and shoved it back into the envelope.

"Well?" Mr. Devine said.

A minor miracle happened.

"I'll think about it," the Major said.

"I'm staying at that little bed and breakfast near the train station," said Mr. Devine. "I'll wait there for your answer."

Mr. Devine left. The Major tucked the envelope into one of his uniform pockets.

"I have to get back to work," he said.

"But—"

"You haven't finished your chores. I expect you to have them done by the time I get home."

"Yes, sir!" I clicked my heels and gave him a crisp salute. For once I wasn't being completely facetious. I wanted him to say yes. I would have given my left arm to get away for a few weeks, even if it meant going to Iceland, wherever that was. I wasn't entirely sure. All I knew was that it wasn't here, the Major wasn't there, and the old man wanted me to go. That was more than enough reason to pack my bags.

I picked up all the clothes from the floor of my room, scooped them into the hamper and carried them downstairs, where I started a load of laundry. I mopped the bathroom floor and the kitchen floor. I ran the vacuum cleaner over the carpet in the living room. I emptied the dishwasher of all the clean dishes and refilled it with the dirty dishes that were piled in the sink. I moved the laundry from the washer to the dryer and put together a casserole while I waited for the dry cycle to finish. By the time the Major reappeared, the casserole was in the oven, the laundry was put away, and I was slicing tomatoes for a salad. The Major, who is usually pretty slick about hiding his feelings, stood in the doorway to the kitchen, briefcase in hand and stared at me in astonishment.

"Supper will be ready in five minutes," I said without turning around.

He disappeared and was back again exactly five minutes later. I'm not kidding. The kitchen timer went off just as he pulled out his chair at the table. He'd showered and changed out of his uniform and into jeans—the only jeans on the planet with a knife-edged pleat down the front of each leg— and a blindingly white T-shirt.

I served him some casserole and passed the salad. We ate in silence for a few minutes. Then he put down his fork and leaned back in his chair.

"I still don't like the idea, Rennie."

The Major isn't precise just with his time and his appearance. Or just with rules and the law. Or tidiness and orderliness. He's also precise— extremely precise—with his choice of words. So my ears pricked up. He hadn't said, "No, and that's that." He had said, "I still don't like the idea."

I knew better than to interrupt. I forked a slice of tomato into my mouth and chewed slowly.

"What kind of man sends teenaged boys all over the world?" the Major said.

"He was like that," I said. "He had this idea that if you get out of your comfort zone and take on something, especially if it's for someone else, you can learn more about yourself in a few days or a few weeks than you ever could in a whole lifetime of just doing the same old cautious thing day in and day out."

"Since when did you ever do the cautious thing?" the Major asked.

"Okay, so maybe he meant that a person has to get out of his rut from time to time. Try something different."

"He told you that?"

I nodded.

"It makes a lot of sense," the Major said.

"You would have liked him. He was a good guy."

"I know."

"What?" I stared at the Major. Like I said, he was precise in his choice of words. He hadn't said, "Maybe," or "I doubt it," or even, "I guess we'll never know." He'd said, "I know."

"I did like him. I liked him a lot. But—"

"You met him?"

"I talked to him."

I remembered. But that conversation had lasted ten minutes, tops. When I said that, the Major fixed me with one of his patented you've-got-to-be-kidding looks.

"My delinquent son disappears, calls me from Toronto after a couple of weeks and tells me he's staying with his grandfather, and I'm *not* going to check out what he's doing there?"

Well, when he put it like that…

"We talked for a couple of hours."

"A couple of *hours*?" That didn't sound like the Major.

"Well, he did most of the talking."

Now *that* sounded right.

"A lot of it was about your grandmother. The rest was about you. He saw a lot in you."

He saw a lot? What did that mean?

"What about school?" the Major asked.

"Huh?"

"You said you enrolled in school. That was true, wasn't it?"

I nodded. "It's semestered. I start in January. I was going to see if I could pick up a few credits in night school in the meantime."

The Major pondered this.

"If you were to do this," he said finally, "if you were to go to Iceland…"

I caught my breath and held it.

"…you'd be careful, right?"

"Yeah. Sure."

"By which I mean, you wouldn't do anything there that you're not allowed to do here—"

"I don't do that stuff anymore." I really didn't. "That's what that whole camp thing was about, right?" Well, okay, so maybe it had started out as an alternative to a juvenile detention center. But they knew what they were doing at that camp. They'd made me think. So had my grandfather. In fact, he'd started me thinking. I took off in the first place because I didn't want to show up for a meeting with my youth worker. I didn't want to hear what he had in mind for me. I'd ended up at my grandfather's because I couldn't think where else to go. We'd talked. And talked and talked. By the time I came home, I'd more or less decided to deal with it. And if that meant spending a few months at boot camp with a bunch of other screwups, okay, I'd do it.

"And use a guide," the Major said. "The lawyer said that's provided for."

"Sure thing."

"And prepare properly. For a thing like this, it's all in the preparation. If you went, you'd be going to a country that's just south of the Arctic Circle."

"Yeah?"

"I know it sounds great, but it can play havoc with your circadian rhythm."

"My what?"

"Your sleep patterns, Rennie. It's also not an easy place to get around. The whole country has maybe 300,000 people in it, and they're scattered around the edges in tiny settlements—the ones that aren't living in the capital, that is. You'd need to drive, and I'm not at all sure you'd be able to rent a car there. Usually you have to be twenty-one for that. We'd probably have to make some other arrangement."

I'd forgotten all about my supper by now. He was talking as if he was going to let me go. Either that or I was dreaming—big time!

The Major sat up a little straighter and looked hard at me from across the table.

"One way or another, you're going to be gone in another year, two at most. You're going to be making all of your own decisions." He paused and looked at me again. "Before you do this, Rennie, I want you to prepare. I want to see your plans. And you have to promise that you'll stay in touch. *D'accord?*"

French. He was speaking French, which he only ever did when he was being dead serious.

"*D'accord, Papa*," I said. I would have agreed with the devil himself to be able to make this trip. "Anything you say."

FIVE

I had just secured the straps on my duffel bag when the Major appeared.

"You have everything?" he asked.

"Yup."

"Sweaters? Longjohns? Parka? Gloves? Hat?"

"Yup, yup, yup, yup, and yup."

"Because the average temperature is maybe seven degrees Celsius—and average doesn't mean that's what it's going to be. It could be—"

"A lot colder or a lot warmer. I know what an average is, thanks," I said, maybe a little too testily considering my math grade.

"Did you remember sunscreen?" he asked. "Just because it's going to be cool, doesn't mean your skin can't burn."

"Got it," I said.

"Hiking boots? If you're going into the interior, you'll need them. The terrain is pretty rough, especially if you run into a lava field—"

"Got 'em." I began to count, slowly, under my breath. Jeez, he was going to drive me nuts.

"Warm socks? Lots of them?"

"Got socks," I assured him. "Here. Here's my list. I checked off everything as I packed it. Why don't you take a look and see if I've forgotten anything?" I hadn't. I'd done my homework and I'd made most of the arrangements myself. Mr. Devine had bought my airline tickets and hired the guide my grandfather had requested.

He seemed surprised, but pleasantly so, which, in turn, was a nice surprise for me. Yeah, I'd learned a few things up there at that camp. I'd paid close attention, mostly (at first) so that I could get the hell out of there as soon as possible. Who would have guessed it, but the stuff they'd taught me actually worked!

"Looks good, Rennie," the Major said when he handed the list back to me. "So, I guess we'd better get you to the airport."

I reached for my duffel bag, but he got to it first and carried it down the stairs and out to the car, where he stowed it in the trunk. We drove to the airport in silence. He stayed with me while I checked in and got my boarding pass and then walked with me to the security gate.

"You let me know when you get there," he said.

"I will."

He reached into his pocket and pulled out something. He handed it to me.

"You told me not to bring my cell phone," I said. He was probably convinced I'd lose it.

"This one is set up to operate there. Just in case."

"Thanks."

He handed me a piece of paper.

"What's this?"

"The name of someone in Iceland you can call if you need anything."

"You know someone in Iceland?"

"Jake does." Jake Thorson was the Major's best buddy. "His mother was Icelandic. That's his Uncle Geir's number. You can call him anytime."

"Is he in the army?"

"He works for one of the daily newspapers there. He's some kind of editor."

I tucked the paper into my jeans pocket.

"Be careful driving over there, Rennie," the Major said. "The temperature and the weather can change just like that." He snapped his fingers. "Be especially careful on gravel. You don't get good traction on gravel."

"I know. I'll be careful."

"And stay off the glaciers. They're dangerous."

"I think part of the reason I'm going is to *see* the glaciers." I'd been online checking out the place. Iceland had the biggest glaciers outside of Greenland and the Antarctic.

"Well, be careful. Really big glaciers can create their own weather systems. Do what your guide tells you. And don't even think about going into an ice cave. I don't know if you know this, but—"

"I know," I said. "You told me at least a dozen times. I'll be careful."

He nodded slowly.

"Okay then. Well…" He looked awkwardly at me.

Then, without warning, I found myself engulfed in a bear hug. "*Sois prudent, mon fils. Bon voyage.*"

"*Au revoir, Papa.*"

The first thing that surprised me was how many people were going to Iceland this time of year. The plane was full, and we were jammed in like cargo. I have long legs, and there was no room for them. My knees became best friends with my chin on the way over. The movie selection sucked—there was nothing first-run and nothing worth seeing a second time. I tried to sleep, but a baby somewhere behind me started to shriek. When I couldn't stand it anymore, I got up to see if I could locate the kid. I had it in mind to make a helpful suggestion or two to the parents. But the parents turned out to be just the mother—she didn't look any older than me—and she was doing her best to shush her baby before some jerk complained. I sat down, put on my earphones, jacked up some Björk, and tried to figure out what kind of country would make someone like her a rock diva. Before long, the baby settled down.

The next thing I knew, we were making our descent into Keflavik airport. Then it was like airports anywhere—get off the plane, stand around to get your luggage, stand around again to be quizzed by a stone-faced customs officer, get your passport stamped, and welcome to Iceland.

I went out through the doors of the customs hall into the arrivals area along with everyone else and peered around, wondering how I was going to recognize Brynja Einarsdottir. I had no idea what he looked like. All I knew was that Mr. Devine had given him my email address and he'd emailed me to tell me he'd meet me at the airport and take me to a guide named Einar Magnusson, who was going to take me to the interior.

I peered around nervously. What if this Brynja and I didn't connect? I realized—too late—that I didn't have a phone number for the guide. I wasn't even sure where he lived, except that it was near some place that sounded like Reykjavik, the capital of Iceland, but wasn't.

It turned out that I had nothing to worry about. As soon as the customs hall doors swooshed shut behind me, I saw a big cardboard sign with my name printed on it in block letters. I walked toward it—and the girl who was holding it.

"I'm Rennie," I said, looking over her shoulder for the guy named Brynja.

"I'm Brynja," she said. I guess the surprise must have showed on my face because she said, "Didn't you get my email?"

"Sure. But..." Some thoughts are better left unfinished. At least, that's what they said at the camp, usually when some guy—usually me—started to say something he wasn't supposed to. Like, say, calling some other guy one of the names that were officially banned.

"But what?"

"Never mind," I mumbled.

"You seem disappointed."

"No." I looked into Brynja's clear blue eyes. She was a little shorter than me, slender, with thick blond hair that hung down over her shoulders. "No, I'm not disappointed. Really."

"Surprised perhaps?" she persisted.

"Well..." I glanced down at the toes of my sneakers. "Maybe a little. I was expecting..."

"What?"

"I thought you'd be a guy."

Her eyes widened. "You're kidding," she said.

I shook my head.

"But I signed the email with my patronymic."

"Huh?"

"My whole name."

"Yeah, but I've never heard of anyone called Brynja before. I thought it was like Bernie, you know? That's a guy's name."

"But it's Brynja *Einarsdottir*," she said, emphasizing the last name as if it was supposed to mean something to me. It didn't. I must have looked pretty blank, because she said, "*Dottir* means daughter."

I thought about that for a second. "So your last name means something like Einar's daughter?"

"That's exactly what it means."

"Wow. What are the chances?" I mean, what *were* the chances?

"Chances?"

"It's like meeting a guy named Luke Robertson who is taking me to meet a guy named Robert. You're Brynja Einarsdottir and you're taking me to meet a guy named Einar."

She let out a long sigh. "You don't know much about Iceland, do you?"

I tried to hold my anger in check. "I did my homework."

"Well, you obviously missed a few things. Most Icelanders don't have last names the way you do in America."

"I'm Canadian," I pointed out.

"Whatever. My name is Brynja. My father's name is Einar. So I am Brynja Einarsdottir. If I had a brother, he would be Einars*son*. My father's father's name was Magnus, so my father is Einar Magnus*son*. *His* father's name was Olaf, so my great-grandfather's name was Tor—"

"Olafsson. I get it," I said. What I thought was, Whatever. "And I'm from Canada, not America."

She shrugged. The look in her eyes said that she either made no distinction or didn't care to make one.

"Is that your only luggage?" she asked, glancing at my duffel bag.

I nodded. Before I could move, she grabbed it and headed for the terminal doors, leaving me with no choice but to trot after her. When the doors swooshed open and a blast of icy wind hit me, I wished I was wearing my parka.

The duffel bag was heavy. I knew that for a fact because I had toted it from the Major's car to the check-in at the airport back home. But she was swinging it along in front of me as if it was a handbag. She wove her way through the parking lot, stopped beside a four-wheel-drive suv and tossed the duffel bag into the rear cargo area. Without even a glance at me, she climbed in behind the wheel and started the engine.

"I'm supposed to have a car," I said through the open passenger-side window.

"My dad has one for you. You have a driver's license, right?"

Jeez, what did she think?

She put the vehicle in gear and glanced inquiringly at me.

I jumped in and hadn't even begun to buckle my seat belt when she stomped on the gas and we shot forward.

"Hey!" It came out automatically.

She chuckled.

I wanted to be mad at her—she had real attitude. Like I was supposed to have known she was a girl, like I should know every damn thing about her country when she obviously knew nothing at all about mine. I hoped I wasn't going to have to spend a lot of time with her. I sincerely hoped she wasn't planning to hike to the interior with me and her father. If she was, I had news for her. After all, my grandfather was paying for this. If that didn't give me the right to say who came and who didn't, then I don't know what did.

We had just got underway when it started to rain—an all-out downpour. Brynja had the windshield wipers going flat out. We drove in silence. There was no way I going to make small talk with a girl driving in a storm. The gray sky and the dismal rain were a perfect match for the fields of black rock on one side of the road and the slate-gray ocean on the other.

The rain stopped suddenly, about the same time a cluster of buildings appeared up ahead.

"Reykjavik," Brynja said. "We're going past it." She glanced at me. "It's good you got here when you did."

"What do you mean?"

"So you can see my *afi*." She glanced at me. "My grandfather."

"What for?" What did her grandfather have to do with anything?

"If it wasn't for him, you wouldn't be here."

"Huh?"

"I mean, you wouldn't even be alive," she said. "You know the story, right?"

"What story?"

She rolled her eyes. I was fast getting the impression that I was a huge disappointment to her—not that I cared. I mean, what did it matter to me what she thought?

"Your grandfather's plane crash-landed in the interior during World War Two."

"Yeah. So?"

"My afi saved his life."

I stared at her. "Your grandfather is the Sigurdur my grandfather told me about?" She nodded. "But I thought—"

Her sigh was downright theatrical. Yeah, she definitely had attitude.

"You thought what?" She made it sound like, *What ridiculous notion popped into your head this time?*

Well, if she was going to be like that...

I took a deep breath. "I thought he died."

Tears welled up in her eyes. Uh-oh.

"What I mean is…my grandfather and yours exchanged cards at Christmas. But last year, my grandfather didn't hear anything, so he assumed…" *When you assume*, my most recent school principal said, *you make an ass out of u and me. Get it, Rennie?*

"He's not dead," she said. Her tone was sharp. Accusatory. I remembered what she had said: that it was good I'd arrived when I did. I hoped that didn't mean what I thought it meant. I also wondered how it might affect what I was supposed to do. Did Mr. Devine know all this when he chose Brynja's father as my guide? Did it matter? "When he heard you were coming, he was so excited," Brynja said. "He wants to meet you."

"Yeah?"

"Yeah." She said it as if she couldn't imagine why. She was quiet for a long time, which was okay by me. Then she said, "Tell me about your grandfather. What was it like growing up around a man who had so many adventures?"

"I don't really know," I said.

"What do you mean, you don't know?"

"I mean, I didn't even know he existed until after my mother died."

She looked at me so sharply and for such a long time that I was sure she was going to miss the turn in the road up ahead.

"Uh, Brynja…" I grabbed the steering wheel. She looked straight ahead, her whole body went rigid for a moment, and she wrenched the wheel, sending gravel cascading down the sharp drop into the sea below. She eased off the gas pedal.

"Sorry," she murmured. "It's just—I didn't know about your mother."

"It's no big deal." That was my standard line. I killed my mother, no biggie, right? But this time, as soon as the words were out of my mouth, I wished I had chosen different ones. Her eyes were hard and her look sharp. "I mean, it's no big deal that you didn't know. Why should you? It was a couple of years ago."

"How did it happen?"

"It was…an accident." That's what they'd called it, a freak accident. Falling rock in Northern Ontario. There were signs posted along the road warning about it, but I'd never heard of it happening and I'd never seen it until that day. We were cruising along, just my mom and me, with the top down on her little convertible. My dad was away, as usual, and we were on a road trip to visit my grandmother, who lived in Toronto. Then, just like that, something crashed right onto the car. I remember hearing it. I remember thinking, Holy %@$#! The car swerved and slammed into the rock face. Despite my seat belt, I hurtled face-first into the airbag. Everything went black. When I finally lifted my head, I looked over at my mom. But all I saw was rock.

"It was an accident," I said again. "It was a long time ago." But I remembered it as clearly as if it had been yesterday.

She didn't say another word. Neither did I. I stared out the window, where there wasn't much to look at except ocean, rock, the occasional farm and sheep. Lots of sheep, all over the place, usually in groups of three. And waterfalls. I'd never seen so many waterfalls.

SIX

We seemed to be moving inland. I heard a bell-like sound. Brynja frowned at the display on the dash. She was low on gas. Forty minutes and another warning ding later, she turned off the main road, and the next thing I knew, we were approaching a small town.

"Borgarnes," she said. "We live between here and Reykholt."

That was it. That was the name of the town I couldn't remember at the airport.

She slowed and pulled into a gas station. She jumped out, grabbed a pump and began to fill up.

I got out to stretch my legs. I was walking toward a tourist information center when I heard someone shout in a language I assumed was Icelandic. I turned and saw Brynja, gas pump in one hand, push a woman away from her. The woman was jabbering at her the whole time and came at her again as soon as Brynja had shoved her. I doubled back, and Brynja pulled up the nozzle and thrust the gas hose at me. The woman was still talking. While I stood there holding the hose, Brynja shoved her again, harder this time, and the woman went flying backward and landed on her butt on the ground. I stared at Brynja. Her face was completely transformed by anger and hatred.

"What's going on?" I said. "Are you okay? Do you—?"

"Get back in the car," she said, grabbing the nozzle from me.

Right. Like some girl I didn't even know was going to start ordering me around as if she was the Major.

Brynja jammed the gas nozzle back into the gas tank and the numbers on the machine started spinning again.

The woman struggled to her feet. Brynja looked at her and hissed something in Icelandic.

The woman turned and said something to me.

"I don't understand," I said.

"Get in the car," Brynja said.

"Please." The woman turned to me and spoke in English this time. "Please, I just want to know where my husband is."

Her husband? I didn't know who this woman was. How was I supposed to know anything about her husband?

"I'm sorry, but I—" I began.

Brynja finished filling the tank. She slammed the nozzle back into its slot and spoke sharply to the woman. To me she said, "I'm going to pay. Get in the car and don't talk to her. She's crazy."

With that, she marched toward the gas station. I circled around to the passenger side. The woman followed me.

"Please," she said. "Please, I know he wouldn't desert me. Please, talk to her. I just want to know where he is."

"Look, lady, I'm not from around here."

She grabbed my hand and held it tightly.

"You look like a good person. Ask her. Just ask her, that's all I want."

I saw Brynja through the window of the gas station. She was holding a mobile phone to her ear while she glared at me.

"Lady, I really have to—"

"She knows. I know she does. Or her father knows. Please."

I glanced back at Brynja. She put the phone back in her pocket and pushed open the gas station door. She wasn't looking at me; she was looking at a car that was pulling into the gas station.

A police car.

It pulled up behind the woman just as Brynja reappeared, and two cops got out.

The one who had been riding shotgun sprang out of the car and strode over to Brynja. Maybe I was reading it wrong, but it seemed to me like he wanted to be the first to get a handle on the situation. He listened for a moment and then turned to the woman and spoke to her. She looked frightened and replied in the same whiny voice she had used on Brynja. The second cop took his time getting out of the car. He was taller than the first one. He watched for a moment before approaching the woman. He bent down and said something into her ear. When he straightened again, she stared up at him. Then she slunk away. She vanished into a grocery store across the street.

"Jeez, what did you say to her?" I asked. He'd gotten action and he'd gotten it fast.

The second cop looked me over. Cops are always doing that—sizing people up before they speak to them. It didn't bother me. I lived with the Major.

"I told her if she made a nuisance of herself again, I'd have a word with her boss. It's a tough economy these days, and it won't be easy for a woman her age to find another job." He spoke even better English that Brynja, with an accent that made me think of New York. Maybe his teacher had been from New York. Or maybe he'd lived there for a while.

Brynja said something in Icelandic.

The first cop scowled his disapproval and spoke angrily.

"What's going on?" I asked.

"I told you to get in the car," Brynja said.

The tall cop grinned. "Sounds like she's got you on a short leash, son."

"Shut up, Karl," Brynja said.

The first cop clucked his disapproval. Brynja growled at him in Icelandic.

"Mind your manners, Brynja," the first cop said in English, glancing at me.

"At least Karl got her to go away," Brynja said. "But you, Tryggvi? You're useless. She only moved here so that she could harass us—and today of all days. But you do nothing."

"The minute she breaks the law, we'll deal with her," Karl said smoothly. Tryggvi shot him an annoyed look. "But she's crazy, not criminal, and everyone knows it. And being crazy is not against the law."

Tryggvi broke in. "She's been warned. If she sets foot on your property again, I'll arrest her for trespassing. Other than that, there's nothing I can do." I noticed he said *I*, not *we*. "She'll eventually give up and accept what happened. She'll have to."

"What happened?" I asked.

"That's none of your business," Brynja said. She opened the driver's-side door. "Get in the car, Rennie." Her tone was warning. She sounded eerily like the Major.

I counted to five before climbing in beside her, so she wouldn't think I was going to jump every time she yelled at me.

"What was that all about?" I asked as she put the engine in gear.

No answer.

"What's with those cops?" I asked instead.

"What do you mean?"

Where should I start? "You talk to cops back home the way you did just now, and they'd bust you out of spite."

"Tryggvi is my uncle."

"You talk to your uncle like that?"

"It's more accurate to say he's my ex-uncle. He used to be married to my father's sister. If you ask me, he's an ass, not to mention an arrogant one. My aunt agrees with me."

"And your dad?"

"You know what men are like. They stick together."

In other words, the brothers-in-law had remained tight.

"Tryggvi thinks he's a big deal because he's a cop and he got his training in America at the FBI."

"He trained at Quantico?" Not bad. If I'd liked cops, which I didn't, I might have been impressed.

"He thought he would come back here and be

made chief of police in Reykjavik. But instead he's stuck here. It drives him crazy."

"And the other one?"

"Karl? Karl drives him even crazier. Tryggvi thinks he doesn't understand the way things work over here. He's always competing with Karl. He says the only reason all the bosses like Karl is because they're so flattered he decided to come back here."

"Back?"

"His grandfather was Icelandic, but Karl's father emigrated before Karl was even born." That explained the American accent. "He spent most of his summers over here when he was a kid. A few years back, he came for a vacation and decided to stay."

"What did he do in the States?"

"He was a cop."

And *that* explained Tryggvi's annoyance. After his time in Quantico, he probably thought he had it all over Karl. But Americans...well, let's just say they never seem short on confidence, and I bet Karl didn't take well to Tryggvi insisting he didn't understand people over here.

We drove in silence for a few moments. I kept waiting for Brynja to explain what had just happened, but she didn't, which meant that I had to take the bull by the horns.

"Brynja, what happened to that woman's husband?"

There was a long pause before she said, "I have no idea. But I sincerely hope he's dead."

She refused to look at me again. I guessed there was no point in asking her what was so important about today of all days.

Fifteen minutes later, we turned onto a graveled laneway and drove across a narrow bridge. We passed a tiny church, a barn and a few other smaller buildings, then stopped in front of a white house with red trim.

"Who lives here?" I asked.

"We do." She spat the words at me. Still angry, I deduced. "My dad, my afi and me."

I considered asking about her mother but, given her mood, decided not to push my luck.

But there was one question I had to ask.

"Um…" I admit it. She had me walking on eggshells and choosing my words carefully so she wouldn't give me more attitude. "Could I maybe settle in first?"

"Settle in?" She spoke the words as if she didn't know what they meant.

"Check into the motel or whatever, take a shower, maybe catch a nap—"

"Motel?" she said. "What motel?" As if she had no idea what I was talking about. See what I mean?

"Hotel, then."

"The hotel in Reykholt is booked up for a conference."

"How about in Borgarnes?"

"You're staying with us until my dad can take you to the interior."

"Yeah, but I—"

"You Americans are so rude. Someone offers you hospitality—"

"I'm Canadian," I said.

She didn't even pause. "—and all you do is complain."

"Fine. Okay."

She crossed her arms over her chest and waited.

"Thank you," I said finally.

"That's the car you can use," she said, pointing to an ancient Yaris in the driveway. "The keys are inside. Come on." She climbed out of the suv, circled around to the back and was halfway to the front door with my duffel bag before I realized what was happening.

"Hey, I can take that," I said.

No response. She shoved open the front door and disappeared inside. I scrambled after her.

The main floor of the house was large and the kind of neat the Major would have approved of. To the right was a living room, to the left a dining room and behind that, a kitchen. All the rooms were painted a gleaming white. Paintings and photographs decorated the walls between and above bookcases crammed with books. The Major had told me that Iceland had one of the highest literacy rates in the world, due to a combination of the long dark winters and the state religion, Lutheranism, which required that all children be able to read and write in order to make their confirmation into the church.

"Come on," she said, still toting my duffel bag as she led me up a flight of stairs and down a hallway to the back of the house. She dropped my bag on the floor of an immaculate room. It, too, was painted white and had a large window that overlooked a meadow and, beyond that, a waterfall that started somewhere in the highlands behind the farm. "This is your room. There's a toilet and shower across the hall. You have it to yourself. You can get cleaned up if you want. I'll be downstairs whenever you're ready to meet my afi."

"What about your dad?"

"He won't be back until the day after tomorrow. He's got a group."

"Group?"

"Of tourists. That's what he does."

"Your dad's a tour guide?"

"Yes." She seemed to dare me to say something about it.

I kept my mouth shut, but what I was thinking was, Terrific, I'm stuck here with an old man and a sour girl. This was not at all what I had expected.

"Okay. Thanks," I said.

I waited until I heard her footsteps going down the stairs. Then I hiked my duffel bag up onto the bed, dug out some clean clothes and changed. Reluctantly, I went back downstairs.

The house was silent.

"Brynja?" I called tentatively.

"Back here."

I followed her voice and found her standing in the doorway to a room behind the kitchen. A woman came out. She had an enormous handbag over her shoulder. Knitting needles poked out of it. She spoke to Brynja in Icelandic, and Brynja listened intently. The woman nodded at me as she passed. Brynja didn't introduce us.

"Come on," she said to me instead.

I followed her into the room.

An old man was lying in a sturdy wood-framed bed that looked enormous in comparison to his shrunken body. But his eyes burned a brilliant and lively blue—Iceland was clearly the land of blue eyes—and his weathered face broke into a nearly toothless smile when he saw Brynja.

"I have a visitor for you, Afi," Brynja said, in English this time.

The old man's eyes shifted to me. He squinted at me and struggled to sit up.

"David? Is that really you?" he said in a quivering voice.

David was my grandfather's name.

Brynja went to the bedside and propped the old man up with pillows.

"No, Afi," she said. "It's not David. His name is Rennie. I told you he was coming. David is his grandfather."

The old man was staring at me the whole time. He said something to Brynja and gestured with a shaky hand to the table under the window beside the bed. Brynja went to it and picked up a silver-framed photograph. She handed it to him, but he waved his hand and said something else.

"He wants you to look at it," she said. She handed it to me.

There were two young men in the photo, both bundled up against the cold, but both faces clearly visible.

"The one on the left is Afi," Brynja said. "The one on the right is your grandfather."

He looked so young. They both did.

The old man said something else.

"He says you look like him," Brynja translated.

I peered at the picture. If you ask me, I didn't look anything like him. But then I never do see resemblances.

When people coo at a tiny baby and says it looks just like its mother or its father, I don't get it. Babies all look like little aliens to me with their big heads, their even bigger eyes, and their bizarre language of gurgles and screams that only their mothers ever understand.

Brynja's grandfather said something else.

"In English, Afi," Brynja said gently. "Rennie doesn't understand Icelandic." To me she said, "Come closer so he can see you and talk to you."

I moved closer to the bed. The old man gestured again, and Brynja pulled a chair over for me to sit on.

"You are David's grandson?" he asked.

"I'm one of them." I was pretty sure that after sixty years of Christmas letters, he knew about the others.

"How is he?" the old man asked.

I glanced at Brynja.

"I told you, Afi. Remember?" she said. The old man looked confused. "He died," Brynja said softly. Tears welled up in her eyes as the smile faded from old man's face.

"I visited him a while ago," I said, mostly because no one else was talking. "I spent nearly a month with him." The old man perked up again, and I told him as much as I could about my grandfather, which turned out to be more than I had realized. Finally the old man asked me what had brought me to Iceland. "He sent me," I said. "He wants me to go to the interior and do something for him."

Naturally, Brynja asked what, and the old man looked at me for an answer.

I wasn't one-hundred-percent sure—and I had no idea why—but from everything that my grandfather had said, I assumed that part of the reason I'd been sent here now was because my grandfather thought this old man was dead.

But he wasn't.

I hesitated.

The old man peered at me, waiting.

What the heck. He had saved my grandfather's life. If anyone had the right to know, he did.

I reached into my pocket, pulled out the little journal and pressed it into his hand.

A phone rang out in the kitchen. Brynja looked over her shoulder in annoyance.

"I'll be right back," she said.

"My grandfather wanted me to leave this there," I said when Brynja had left. "He told me exactly where to go."

The old man opened the book and squinted at it. He groped for something on his bedside table—eyeglasses. I picked them up and gave them to him. He put them on and flipped through the pages, looking at the sketches. Tears welled up in his eyes. His hands trembled.

"Who did this belong to?"

"My grandfather. He said she—"

The old man looked so sharply at me that I stopped immediately. He snapped the journal shut. What had I done? Something that upset him, that was for sure. I knew then that I was right and that my grandfather had wanted this done now because he thought the old man had died. I wished—not for the first time in my life—that I'd kept my mouth shut.

But that wasn't why the old man stopped reading the journal. He was looking over my shoulder. I turned and saw that Brynja had returned. She said something in Icelandic.

He shook his head and said, "Brynja, leave us."

She started to protest, but he spoke to her again. She scowled at me as if it were my fault—which it kind of was—and left the room. He called to her again, and she shut the door behind her.

Then he leaned toward me as best he could.

"You know who this is?" he asked, opening the journal again and holding up the sketch of the woman.

"I know a little," I said.

"You must not say anything to Brynja," the old man said. "Or her father. You must not let them see that book. Do you understand?"

"Sure, but—"

He grasped my hand and squeezed it tightly.

"You must promise me."

His grip was far stronger than I'd expected, and I guessed he had once been a powerful man.

"I promise," I said.

"You must swear it."

Swear it?

"Swear," he hissed at me. "Swear."

I swore I wouldn't say anything to either Brynja or her father or show them the journal.

He slumped back against his pillows and closed his eyes. I waited, but other than the gentle rise and fall of his chest, I saw no movement. He was asleep.

I crept out of the room.

Brynja was waiting for me in the kitchen, arms crossed over her chest, a scowl on her face.

SEVEN

"He's asleep," I said.

Brynja marched out of the kitchen and down the hall to the front of the house.

"What was that about?" she demanded.

"I can't tell you."

"He's *my* afi."

"And it's up to him who he wants to tell things to."

"Why would he tell you something that he didn't tell me?" She was so angry that she was shaking.

"I have no idea." I really didn't. "But if you have any questions about what your grandfather wants, you should ask him."

"Okay, then show me that book."

"I can't do that either."

"Why not?" One thing I was noticing about her: the angrier she got, the louder she got.

"Because it's not up to me. It's up to him."

She glared at me for a few more seconds before turning and stomping back into the kitchen. I thought she was going to roust the old man, but instead I heard cupboards opening and pots clanging. I glanced at my watch. It was late. She was probably making supper.

I wasn't sure what to do. I wasn't sure either what I had got myself into when I agreed to come here, especially after the old man reacted the way he did. What was he hiding? Did my grandfather even know?

I went into the kitchen and asked Brynja if she needed help. She ignored me. I said if she was cooking on my account, she shouldn't bother, that I would take care of myself and didn't want to put her to any trouble. She still ignored me. I left the house, got into the battered Yaris, found the key and drove over the bridge and out onto the road. I headed for Borgarnes, found a restaurant and ordered a hamburger and

78

fries—just like back home. After that I drove around some more and tried to decide what to do next. I didn't particularly want to face Brynja again, but I didn't have much choice. Her father would be back the day after tomorrow. With any luck, he could take me to the interior and I could get my mission over with and be on the plane back home by the end of the week.

I drove back to the house and tried the door. The knob was wrenched out of my hand before I could turn it, and there was Brynja.

"Where were you?" she demanded. "It's late."

"Were you worried?"

Her face turned red. I grinned. "You were, weren't you?" I said.

"I was not! But my father called and—"

"*He* was worried?"

"He is being paid to make sure you are safe while you're here," she said. "You didn't say where you were going. It's dark, and you don't know your way around."

"I got back safe and sound, didn't I? So you can tell your dad he doesn't have to worry. I can take care of myself." I took a step forward, and she retreated just enough to let me into the house. I started for the stairs.

"Rennie?" For once her voice was soft. "I'm sorry I got angry with you."

"It's okay."

"It's just that my afi and I are very close."

"Really, it's okay," I said. To my surprise, she didn't argue with me. Maybe she actually was sorry. "Hey, Brynja, you know that woman from the gas station? What's her story? How come she seems to think you and your dad know where her husband is?" And how come, I thought but didn't ask, you wish the poor guy was dead?

She smiled sweetly. "I'll tell you," she said, "if you show me that book."

Nice try.

"You know I can't do that, Brynja."

The sweet smile vanished.

"Fine, then I can't answer your questions either."

"Whatever."

I went up to bed.

I woke to an eerily quiet house. I dressed quickly and went downstairs. There was no sign of Brynja. I crept upstairs again and checked the other rooms on the second floor. Besides mine, there were two bedrooms and a second bathroom. All were empty. I went back down to the kitchen. Still no Brynja. I knocked softly at the old man's door. There was no answer. I pushed it open a crack. He was asleep—at least, I hoped he was. I waited until I saw the gentle rise and fall of his chest beneath the blankets. Then I opened another door off the kitchen. It led into a small office. Besides the desk, filing cabinets and bookshelves, there was a computer and printer. I stepped inside for a closer look. The desktop icons looked familiar and included an Internet search connection. But it wasn't my computer, and Brynja might pop in at any moment.

I went back into the kitchen and started opening cupboards to see if there was any cereal.

There wasn't.

I tried the fridge and found eggs, bread and containers of something called skyr. I opened one

and sniffed it. It smelled okay. Then I grabbed a
spoon and tasted some. It was yogurt. I spooned some
into a dish, dropped some bread into a toaster on the
counter and grabbed a couple of eggs. While the eggs
fried and the toast toasted, I ate the skyr. Not bad.
Then I tucked into the second course. I washed all my
dishes and put them away.

There was still no sign of Brynja.

I decided to take a walk. This time I was smart
enough to put on my parka. I should have pulled on a
tuque too. The wind whipped my ears until they hurt.

The outbuildings all looked as neat and well main-
tained as the house. A couple of the smaller ones—
storage sheds of some kind, I guessed—had been
built right into the earth. At least, that was the way
it looked. It probably had something to do with the
shortage of wood way back when. That was an interesting fact I'd picked up in my Internet research.
Until relatively recently, the largest source of wood
in Iceland had been driftwood. That's because the
early settlers—Vikings, mostly—cut down most of
the trees to build houses or to burn to keep warm or
to fuel the fires needed to make iron. Now only one
percent of the land was forested. There was a woodlot

on the other side of the little river that Brynja had driven over to get to the house. It didn't look very big, but it climbed gently up the slope to the base of the highlands. I glanced at the far side of the house, but there was nothing but a large grassy yard with a long narrow rise in the middle of it. Beyond that was a fence, more meadow and a small stream.

I had just finished taking in everything on the property when I saw a car come over the bridge. It pulled up in front of the house and a woman— not Brynja—got out. It was the old man's nurse. She waved to me and went inside.

I still had nothing to do, so I decided to take a run into Borgarnes and poke around there.

Parking was no problem. I found a place outside a small restaurant. From there I walked up and down the few streets, discovering a tourist shop that sold Icelandic sweaters, mitts and hats; a bakery; a pizzeria; a burger joint with a variety store attached; a small art gallery with a café; and a tourist information center. I wandered in there to pick up a few brochures and thought about using one of the computers to get online. But it sounded expensive— five hundred krónur for thirty minutes, when all

I wanted to do was see what was what out here. It wasn't that important. I asked for a map of the area and then headed back to the car. I was about to get in when someone behind me said, "Excuse me."

I turned.

It was the crazy woman from the gas station.

"Look, lady—" I began.

"I'm sorry," she said. She sounded pretty normal. "I hope I didn't upset you yesterday. But they won't tell me where he is, and I know they know."

"They?"

"Einar and Brynja."

I remembered what Brynja had said about the missing man.

"Einar and Brynja know where your husband is and they won't tell you?" That seemed to be what she was saying, but what kind of sense did it make? "Why wouldn't they tell you if they knew?"

"Because they think he killed Gudrun."

"Gudrun?"

The woman's expression changed. She looked confused.

"I thought you and Brynja…"

"Me and Brynja what?"

84

"I'm sorry," she said. "I thought—it doesn't matter. I'm sorry." She turned to go.

"Wait," I said.

She turned slowly.

"Who is Gudrun?"

She shook her head and walked away.

I ran to catch up to her.

"Who is Gudrun? What happened to her?"

She walked more quickly, darting across the street and disappearing into the grocery store. I was about to chase after her when a police car blocked my path.

The window of the car whirred down to reveal Brynja's Uncle Tryggvi, the cop.

"Is that woman bothering you again?" he asked.

"No. Not at all. She just apologized for yesterday."

Tryggvi glanced around. "Where's Brynja?"

"She's busy. I decided to look around, see if there are any sights worth seeing."

"I can give you some ideas, if you want."

"Sure." He took the map from me and circled a couple of nearby destinations.

"It's a beautiful country," he said. "There is a lot to see that you can't see back in America."

"I'm Canadian."

He didn't correct himself but instead started to roll up his window.

"Who's Gudrun?" I said.

The window stopped its ascent.

"There are many Gudruns in Iceland."

"Who's the Gudrun that that woman's husband supposedly killed?"

"Is that what she told you?"

I nodded.

"Gudrun Njalsdottir was a reporter for a newspaper in Reykjavik."

"Until someone killed her," I said.

Tryggvi raised an eyebrow. "Until she died."

"So she wasn't murdered?"

"She fell over a waterfall. It was probably an accident, but her family thinks she was murdered."

"Probably?"

He stared at me as if wondering what business it was of mine. "The death was ruled *Undetermined*," he said. "She drowned. But whether it was an accident or a suicide—"

"Or murder," I said.

"Or homicide," he said, correcting me, "could not be determined."

"But her family thinks she was murdered by that woman's husband?"

"There was an investigation, of course. Then her husband disappeared."

"Disappeared?"

"Left the country. Left his wife behind. She thinks he was the victim of foul play, but we don't have any evidence of that."

"So why does she think Brynja knows where he is?"

Tryggvi examined me silently from behind the wheel of his car. "You're an inquisitive fellow," he said finally. "Is there some special reason you're asking all these questions?"

"The woman harassed Brynja. She came up to me today. She seems to think I can help her."

Tryggvi shook his head. "This is a peaceful country. Unlike America, the homicide rate is low—one or two people a year at most. And the murderers generally turn out to be mentally deranged."

"You mean like that woman?"

"I'm not saying that. But she's clearly upset by the disappearance of her husband. Maybe he got tired of her. Maybe he got tired of Iceland. I don't know."

"So why does she think Brynja knows anything about it?"

"Maybe you should ask her. In the meantime, if that woman gets to be a nuisance, let me know."

I said I would. He wished me a good day, rolled up my window and eased his car on down the street.

The woman was still watching me from inside the grocery store.

EIGHT

I thought about the tourist information center and its Internet connection. Then I remembered the computer in the little office at the back of Brynja's house. If Brynja still wasn't home…

Fifteen minutes later, I let myself in the front door and stood for a moment, listening.

Nothing.

I went through to the kitchen. The door to the old man's room was open and the nurse was inside, knitting beside his bed. I nodded to her. She nodded back. I went through to the back room and sat down at the desk. The computer was still on. I opened Google and it came up looking exactly as it always did back home. I typed in *Gudrun + Njalsdottir + waterfall + death*.

It didn't get me many pages. I clicked through them one by one. Finally, I saw a reference to a Gudrun Njalsdottir who had been found drowned at the base of a waterfall about a year ago. Just as Tryggvi had said, she'd been a reporter specializing in investigative reporting. There was a photograph. She was a gorgeous, dark-haired woman with piercing eyes. The article said an investigation was ongoing. I searched again and found a follow-up article, which said that the investigation had ruled out foul play. There was no mention of murder. There wasn't even a hint of murder, even though Tryggvi had said the family believed someone had killed her. What had made them think that?

"What do you think you're doing?"

Brynja's voice behind me made me jump. I clicked back to Google and cleared the search history.

"I was going to email my dad," I said. She must have been in the doorway to the room when she spoke because she was halfway across the room now. "It's okay if I use this computer, right?"

"You should ask first."

"I would have, but there was no one to ask. I couldn't find you."

She was peering at the screen.

"I just logged on," I said. One thing my past had taught me to do reasonably well was lie. The Major never believed me—well, almost never—but most other people did.

Brynja looked deep into my eyes. Good luck, I thought. Finally she said, "I guess it's okay."

I logged into my email account and sent a brief message to the Major to back up my story.

"So, what are you up to today?" I asked when I'd finished.

"I'm supposed to show you around." She didn't try to hide her lack of enthusiasm.

"I can look after myself if you have something else you'd rather do," I said.

"You're proud of that, aren't you?"

Huh?

"You keep telling me you can look after yourself." It seemed to irritate her.

"Well, I can."

"My father wants me to show you some of the sights, so that's what I'm going to do. Just give me a chance to check my email and get changed."

I nodded and retreated to the kitchen to get myself some Icelandic yogurt. I wasn't sure, but I didn't think Brynja believed that I'd just been sending an email. I think she wanted to find out what sites I had been looking at. Well, good luck with that too.

She was frowning when she went through the kitchen to go upstairs.

"I'll meet you outside," she said. "I won't be long."

I said okay and listened as she went up the stairs. I walked to the front door, opened it and closed it again, loudly. Then I crept upstairs and down the hallway to my left.

"Looking for something?" I asked from the doorway to my room.

It was Brynja's turn to jump.

She whirled around, red-faced.

"Any particular reason you're going through my duffel bag?" I asked.

"I—I…"

"I don't know what you call it here, but back home it's called snooping, and people don't like it."

She didn't say anything.

"So, are you going to change?" I said. "Or are you ready to go?"

"I'm ready."

I followed her to her suv. She didn't say a word about me using the computer, and I didn't say anything about her going through my stuff.

I had no idea what she was like with her friends or her family, but with me she acted like an automated tour guide, complete with phony-perky voice and fake frozen smile. She took me to a couple of waterfalls and hiked me through a lava field that was filled with all kinds of weird rock formations. Then we went up the side of a dormant volcano, and finally she walked me down to a black sand beach that, according to her, had caused a lot of ships to run aground over the years. The sailors had mistaken the blackness of the sand for the blackness of deep water.

"Are you hungry?" she asked me after we had hiked and viewed pretty much everything the area had to offer.

The thing about me: I'm always hungry. My mom used to tease me about having a hollow leg. I felt something stab my heart. It happened all the time. I'd be cruising along, then something would remind me of my mom, and I'd feel the pain all over again.

We got back into her vehicle and drove until we reached a cluster of buildings, including a restaurant. We went in and found a table.

"They have the same kind of food you're used to back home," she said. "Hamburgers, pizza, stuff like that. Or, if you're feeling adventurous…" She paused and looked at me. "Never mind. They do an okay hamburger, not that I've ever had McDonald's or anything."

"I never go to McDonald's," I said. "I prefer to eat healthy." I picked up the menu and looked it over. Besides the burgers, fries and pizza she had mentioned, there were a lot of different kinds of fish and lamb.

"Do you want me to order for you?" she asked.

"I can manage."

A waitress approached. Brynja ordered in Icelandic. The waitress turned to me.

I'd narrowed my choices down to lamb and shark, but I couldn't decide which to order. So I asked the waitress. She glanced at Brynja. Maybe she didn't understand English. Sure enough, she said something to Brynja in Icelandic.

"You can have shark as an appetizer," Brynja said. "They have a dish called *hakarl*. You can have smoked lamb for your entrée."

Sounded good.

Brynja ordered for me.

My shark arrived first—little cubes of it on a plate.

"Go ahead," Brynja said.

I skewered a piece and popped it into my mouth. I gagged as soon as it was in my mouth. It tasted like motor oil, not that I've ever actually tasted motor oil. You know what I mean.

"An Icelandic delicacy?" I asked as soon as I could speak.

"Roughly translated, it's putrefied shark," she said with a smile.

"Putrefied?"

"It gives you stamina." She also said she never ate it.

My lamb arrived about the same time that I smelled cigarettes. "Are you allowed to smoke in restaurants over here?"

Brynja looked surprised. "You smoke?"

"No. But it smells like someone does." I glanced around, but there wasn't a cigarette, lit or otherwise, in sight. I sliced some of the lamb and popped it into my mouth.

Holy crap!

"This tastes like cigarettes," I said. I spit the meat into my napkin.

"It's smoked lamb," Brynja said. "It's also an Icelandic specialty. My grandfather loves it. He has it every year for Christmas."

"Yeah, well, no zoffence, but if you blindfolded me and asked me to lick the bottom of an ashtray, I wouldn't be able to tell the difference between that and this lamb."

"Maybe I should have ordered *hrutspunga*," she said.

"Which is?"

"Ram's testicles."

I gulped. Thank god she hadn't.

The waitress returned. "She wants to know if everything is okay," Brynja said. "And before I answer, I should tell you that it's extremely rude not to eat the food that's put in front of you. In fact, it would be an insult to the chef."

One thing Brynja didn't know about me—
I had eaten boot camp food all summer. I smiled up
at the waitress.

"Can I get a soda, please?"

Brynja stared at me as I tucked into the lamb.
Brynja's meal arrived a minute later: a burger and fries.
She smiled sweetly as she dipped a fry in mayo and
popped it into her mouth.

I cleaned my plate just to show her…well, something. I'm not actually sure what. Brynja and the
waitress had a good chat when Brynja went to pay
the bill.

"You two sound like you're great friends," I said.

"We go to school together."

Oh.

"What if I hadn't ordered smoked lamb and
putrefied shark?" I asked. "Then what?"

"She would have brought them no matter what
you ordered, and I would have told you that they
were the correct dishes."

"You don't like me much, do you?"

"Tell me what my afi said."

"Ask him yourself. And stay out of my room."

We drove back to her place in silence.

There was a helicopter in one of the fields beside Brynja's house. Brynja smiled when she saw it. She jumped out of the car and ran into the house. I followed.

A muscular man in jeans and a sweatshirt was standing in front of some shelves in the living room, straightening the spines of books and the knickknacks in front of them. He turned when he heard us come in.

"*Fadir!*" Brynja said, launching herself into his arms.

The man smiled and hugged her back. He looked over the top of her head at me.

"You must be Rennie," he said. I couldn't help noticing that he spoke with an accent, whereas Brynja's English was almost perfect. He released Brynja and came across the room to shake my hand. "I am Einar," he said.

Brynja said something I didn't understand.

"Brynja, manners," her father chided. "We have a guest. You must speak English."

Brynja scowled at me. She was in no mood to do me any favors. But her father was another story.

"You're back early," she said.

"The clients' son was unruly," Einar said. "Whenever we went hiking, he went so far ahead that I lost track of him. His father kept saying I should not worry because his son was an Eagle Scout back in America. I kept telling the father, America isn't Iceland. When we got to Vatnajökull, the kid disappeared."

"Vatnajökull is a glacier," Brynja told me. "It's the largest one in Europe."

"Eight thousand square kilometers," Einar said. "And this kid decides to take a hike all by himself. We ended up having to send out a search party. He'd fallen into a crevice."

"Was he okay?"

"He broke his ankle. He was down there for a couple of hours before we found him—after dark, I might add. He was lucky. The door swung a little too close to the heel for my liking." Einar must have noticed the giant question mark on my face. "When the door swings too close to the heel, it's what you might call a close call."

Oh.

He shook his head in disgust. "I'll never understand these young boys. I tell them over and over, glaciers are dangerous. Ice is dangerous. You could slip into a crevice and never be seen again. But they all think they're invincible. Americans are the worst."

Brynja shot me a look, as if her father had just proved a point that she'd been arguing with me.

"I'm Canadian," I said—again.

Einar smiled at me. "Has Brynja been taking good care of you?"

"She's shown me a few things," I said.

"Good. Good. I have some business to wrap up in the next day or so, and then we can get organized for your expedition."

"When do you think we'll be able to leave?"

"If all goes well, Thursday," he said.

Thursday? This was only Monday. What was I going to do for the next couple of days?

He must have read the disappointment on my face, because he said, "Have you visited Reykjavik yet?"

I shook my head.

"You must spend a day there. We'll arrange it." He looked at Brynja and held up a picture frame. "I found this facedown. What happened to it?" His tone was mild, but his eyes were sharp and piercing.

Brynja looked at the frame. "I did that yesterday," she said. "I'm sorry, Dad. I just…I'm sorry."

Einar pulled his daughter close and hugged her. "It's all right," he said. "I was thinking about her too." He set the frame back on the shelf. "Well, I'd better unpack."

"I'll help you," Brynja said. She glanced at me. I would have bet anything that what she really wanted to do was tell her dad about the mysterious journal I had shown her grandfather. But that was her business, not mine. Anyway, I had other things on my mind. I was staring at the photograph that Einar had just replaced on the shelf. The woman smiling out at me was eerily familiar. I'd seen her face on the Internet only yesterday. She was Gudrun Njalsdottir, the woman whose family was convinced she had been murdered.

NINE

I woke with the sun. The clock beside my bed read *6:15*. I couldn't get back to sleep—and, believe me, I tried. So I swung up out of bed, showered and got dressed.

The house was quiet. I hesitated to go into the kitchen in case I disturbed the old man. Instead, I let myself out of the house into the crisp morning air and took a stroll around the property. I walked back as far as the base of the waterfall and gazed up at the highlands where it originated. There was a rough path up one side of the falls. I started to climb it. The higher I went, the more spectacular the view became and the colder it got. The farmhouse, the little church and the outbuildings below got smaller and smaller, and once I was at the top, I spotted another farm to the east and Reykholt to the west. The terrain up top was desolate. In the distance, cresting the highest points, was a sheet of white—snow. Or ice. I wasn't sure which. There wasn't a tree anywhere. I don't know why, but it popped into my mind that a fugitive would have a hard time in Iceland. Not only was the place small, but there didn't seem to be anywhere to hide. It was all farmland, coastline and lava fields.

I wandered inland, sticking to the creek so I wouldn't lose my bearings. I was no Eagle Scout, but I knew how to be careful in unfamiliar surroundings—not like, say, Worm, who stepped off the trail to take a leak the day after I duct-taped him to the canoe and promptly got lost. He wasn't my buddy that day; Jimi had had the pleasure, and Jimi hadn't cared that he was gone because we were staying camped for a few days and were only hiking to an old fire tower. Long story short: we spent six hours doing a systematic search for Worm and found him blubbering under a tree just before sundown. He'd gone just far enough into the woods so that he couldn't see the trail and had got disoriented. It happens.

One tree looks pretty much like another, especially to a city boy like Worm.

I followed the creek back to where the waterfall began its tumble to the rocks below. My stomach was growling by then, and I was hoping that Einar at least would be up and ready for breakfast when I got back to the house.

He was.

I spotted him down below.

He was walking around the long narrow rise in the land on the far side of the house from the outbuildings. As I began my descent, I saw him standing in front of the rise. Then I lost track of him. Going down sounds easier than going up, but it isn't, not when you're basically rock climbing in reverse. You have to watch what you're doing and test your footing with each step. It took a good half hour before I got to the bottom. By then Einar was nowhere to be seen.

I found him talking on the phone in the kitchen and started to back away. I didn't want to interrupt his coversation or give him the impression I was trying to eavesdrop either—not that I understood a word of what he was saying—but he turned and saw me. "He's here," he said into the phone, in English this time.

"I'll talk to you later." He closed his phone and set it down onto the counter. "I thought we'd lost you," he said. "Where were you?"

"I woke up early. I guess my internal clock is all screwed up. Everyone was asleep, so I went for a walk. I climbed up by the waterfall. I got a great view from up there."

"You shouldn't wander off without telling anyone where you are."

"Sorry," I muttered.

"Well." He let out a long sigh. "Are you hungry?"

"Starving."

Finally, a smile. "As I suspected. Teenaged boys are always hungry. How about some muesli and yogurt, followed by eggs, toast, cheese, some ham…?"

I grinned as the menu got longer.

"What can I do to help?" I asked.

I had just polished off a bowl of cereal and yogurt, two soft-boiled eggs and three pieces of toast with slices of cheese and ham, when Brynja stumbled into the room.

"Hungry?" Einar asked.

She shook her head. "Is there coffee?"

"Just made. Pour some for Rennie too. I'm going to check on Sigurdur."

He disappeared into the old man's room, leaving me alone with Brynja. She filled a mug of coffee and slammed it down so hard in front of me that it sloshed over the brim.

"Hey!" I ducked back so none would drop onto my jeans. I grabbed a napkin and sopped up the mess on the table.

"Sorry," she said without a shred of sincerity. She took her coffee into the back room and sat down at the computer.

Her father came out of the old man's room. "If I make some tea for Sigurdur, will you sit with him until Elin comes?" he asked Brynja. I guessed Elin was the nurse.

"I'm supposed to meet Johanna," Brynja said. "We have plans."

"I'll stay with him," I said. "I don't have any plans except a shower and a little sightseeing."

Einar looked at me as if weighing both my offer and my character.

"It's really Brynja's responsibility," he said, shooting a disapproving look her way.

"But I already told Johanna," Brynja said. "She'll be here any minute to pick me up. And you heard Rennie. He doesn't have plans."

"Really, I don't mind," I said again.

Einar scowled at Brynja.

"Thank you, Rennie," he said finally. "I appreciate it."

"No problem."

I heard car tires crunching over gravel. Brynja gulped down her coffee and dropped her mug into the sink.

"That's Johanna, "Brynja said. "She's going to borrow an outfit and then we're leaving." The doorbell rang, an Brynja ran to answer it.

Einar put the kettle on and tidied the kitchen while he waited for it to boil. He made a cup of tea.

"You'll have to wait until it cools a little," he said. "And you'll have to help him with it." He stood in front of the stove for a moment and glanced from me to the old man's room as if he was having second thoughts about leaving me to care for him.

"It's no problem, really," I said. "I worked at a nursing home for a couple of months last year. I'm used to old people." I didn't see any point in mentioning that the work was court ordered, part of my sentence for throwing apples at an old man who threatened to call the cops on me because I had stolen "said apples," as the judge called them, from the old guy's tree. The old guy told the judge that I had no respect for my elders. The judge agreed and came up with what he thought would be an appropriate cure.

At first I hated being around so many super-old people. They smelled funny. They looked and talked funny when they didn't have their dentures in. They never heard anything you said the first time. They repeated themselves constantly. They were just taking up space. At least, that's what I had thought at first. The main thing I discovered? Old people can really surprise you. They know stuff you could never in a million years guess they know when all you do is look at them. Like the old guy who'd been a sword swallower in the circus, and another guy who had done one of the first heart transplants in Canada and could still describe it in gory detail.

"Really, he'll be fine," I said. "I won't do anything stupid."

He looked at me a few moments longer.

"Elin should be here in under an hour," he said. "I'd stay myself, but I have to deal with the insurance company, thanks to that boy wandering off on his own and breaking his ankle."

"No problem. Give me your cell number and I'll call you if there's any problem."

He liked that idea. I think he thought it showed responsibility. He jotted it down for me and left.

The old man's eyes were closed when I took the tea into his room. I didn't have the heart to wake him, so I set the tea on his bedside table and sat down to wait. The nurse showed up before the old man's eyes opened. I told her where the family was and got up to leave.

"Has he eaten anything?" Elin asked.

"I don't think so." I hesitated. "What's wrong with him?" I asked. "Is it just because he's old?"

"You mean his illness?"

I nodded.

"Well, he's ninety-seven," she said. "He gave up his practice decades ago." Grandpa's letter had mentioned that Sigurdur had been a doctor. "But he didn't give up farming until last year. Everything stopped for him when his granddaughter died."

"Brynja had a sister?"

"Brynja calls Sigurdur *afi*, but he's really her great-grandfather."

"So his granddaughter was…?"

"Brynja's mother."

"Gudrun?"

She nodded. "He was heartbroken after what happened to her. She drowned, just like her father. It happened just over a year ago—in fact, I think it was a year ago on Sunday." The day I had arrived in Iceland. The day that woman had harassed Brynja at the gas station. That day, of all days.

"Gudrun's father drowned too?" Talk about a hard-luck family!

"Yes, but not the same way as Gudrun. Njal was a fisherman. It's a tough job at the best of times. He went out one day and never came back. Sigrid, Gudrun's mother, was already very ill. Cancer. Gudrun was just a little thing when she died. I think she was five. Sigurdur raised her. He doted on her. Sigrid was his only daughter. Gudrun was his only granddaughter. Now there's just Brynja."

A trembling voice called from the bed. Elin smiled.

"It seems my patient is awake. Excuse me."

I headed upstairs to have a shower. As I peeled off my clothes, I decided I would take a ride into Reykjavik later and poke around. It was the biggest city in Iceland. There had to be something going on. Or maybe I could do a little sightseeing on my own. I was thinking over my options when I got into the shower. I reached for the shampoo and cursed silently. I'd left it in my room.

I opened the shower door, leaving the water running, grabbed a towel, and hot-footed it back to my room.

I don't know who was more startled: me, at finding someone going through my things—*again*— or the would-be thief who was bent over the open drawers of the dresser in my room and who clearly hadn't expected to be interrupted while the shower was still running.

TEN

"Find what you're looking for this time?" I asked, even though I could see that she was lifting the journal out of my bag.

To her credit—well, sort of—she didn't try to hide it.

"What is this?" She held it up and looked at me the way a queen would look at some lowly subject she was about to order beheaded.

"What would your grandfather say if he found out you were snooping where you don't belong?"

"What would he say if he found out you betrayed his trust and told me about this journal?"

"We'll never know, because that's not going to happen. Hearing about your little thieving expedition, however…"

"He won't believe you."

"You sound pretty sure of that," I said. She looked sure too.

"My afi knows that *I* would never betray a trust," she said.

She was nervy, I'll give her that. There she was, doing what she wasn't supposed to be doing and telling me that the old man would never believe it.

"You're a piece of work," I said. "You act all sweet and innocent around your grandfather, and then you go behind his back and snoop into something when he's already made it clear he doesn't consider it any of your business."

"And I suppose it's *your* business?" Her tone was one-hundred-percent pure distilled snottiness.

"Someone made it my business." Oh. "That's what bugs you, isn't it? It's not about who it is. It's about me knowing something that you don't. It's driving you crazy."

"If you say anything to my grandfather, I'll tell him that you told me. He'll never believe you. Never."

Whatever, I told myself. This family's problems were not my problems.

So how come I was so angry? How come all I wanted to do was get even with her? How come that's exactly what I set out to do after she collected Johanna from her room and left—and after I watched them drive away?

I shoved the journal in the glove compartment of the Yaris and headed for the grocery store near the gas station. When I didn't see the woman who had accosted me on my second day in the country, I described her to the closest cashier.

"Oh," said the brassy blond. "You must mean Freyja."

"The same Freyja who's been trying to find her husband?"

"That's what they say. I don't know her very well. She's only been working here for a couple of weeks, and she keeps to herself. But someone said that her husband ran off with a co-worker or a lover or something and that Freyja hasn't been right in the head since."

"Is she working today?"

She shook her head.

"Do you know where I can find her?"

"She rents a room from Halbjorn—he has the blue house at the end of town. I guess she would be there on her day off."

Freyja was there, all right. She was coming around the side of the house with a calico cat in her arms.

"Excuse me," I said, smiling in what I hoped was a non-threatening way. "Freyja?" It felt funny calling her by her first name, but when I'd asked the cashier for her last name, she'd said simply, "Her name is Freyja." Brynja hadn't been kidding. People really did call each other by their first names.

Freyja froze when she saw me.

"Remember me from the gas station?" I said. "I was with Brynja. I'm Rennie."

She looked over my shoulder as if she expected to see Brynja or maybe the cops. When they didn't appear, she still looked tense.

"I wanted to ask you about your husband," I said.

"Baldur? You want to ask me about Baldur? Did someone send you? Is this a trick?"

"No one sent me." I stepped closer and tried to pet the cat. It hissed at me. I backed off. "You asked me to talk to Brynja about him. Why? What do you think she knows?"

"She knows where he is. They both know."

"So why won't they tell you?"

"Because they have hatred in their hearts, and it has turned them evil."

I stared at her. She spoke calmly enough, but there was a bite to her voice. I wondered if Brynja was right: this woman was crazy.

The sky overhead was lead gray, and a whipping wind had come up since I'd left the house. I shivered inside my jacket.

"I don't understand," I said.

"They think he killed Gudrun, and they think I know it."

"Why do they think that?" I asked.

"I don't know. All I know is that he didn't do it. My Baldur would never kill anyone."

"Mrs…uh…Freyja, I don't understand. Why would anyone think your husband killed Gudrun?"

"They blame him for what happened. After she died, he used to stand outside our house and shout

116

that Baldur was a murderer." He? Did she mean Einar? "He told everyone who would listen that Baldur killed his wife. He said he wasn't going to let Baldur get away with it. And Brynja—she…"

"She what?"

"Brynja was in the same class as my daughter. She made Rakel's life miserable until she couldn't stand it anymore. She's living with her aunt and uncle and going to school in Denmark. She says she never wants to come home again."

I wondered why Freyja didn't leave as well. She would probably be a lot happier in Denmark than she was here.

"Why don't you tell me what happened?" I asked.

Her gold-brown eyes were rimmed with black smudges as if she hadn't slept well in days or even weeks.

"Do you really want to know?"

"I do." I had nothing else going on, and I wanted to know whatever it was that Brynja refused to tell me.

Freyja stroked the cat. She started toward the house.

"Come in," she said.

I followed her into a small but tidy house and up a narrow flight of stairs to a room at the back.

It was filled with the morning sun and was larger than I expected. To one side, there was a small fridge, a few feet of counter, and both an electric kettle and an electric coffee pot. The smell of strong coffee filled the little room.

She asked me to sit. She opened a cupboard and took out a couple of cake tins. She sliced some cake from the first one. From the second, she produced some cookies, which she set on a plate with the cake. She set it on the coffee table in front of the small sofa, poured the coffee and asked me how I liked mine. She handed me my cup and settled into a chair opposite me.

"Baldur used to own a fishing boat," she said. "A big one. Very modern. When things were going well a few years back, when the boom was on, he decided he wanted to try something different. It was so easy to get loans then, not like today. The banks were practically giving money away."

A bank *giving* money away? She had to be kidding!

"What I mean to say is," she continued, "that it was easy to get a loan and the interest rates were low. So Baldur took out a big loan and used his fishing quota as collateral. He used some of the money to improve the house and to get nice things for me and Rakel.

But most of it he used for his big dream. He wanted to build a condominium resort for rich local people and wealthy tourists. It would have a beautiful setting, luxury accommodations, excellent restaurants, entertainment, a casino, all the amenities a person could wish for. It would bring jobs and money into the economy. He had people who were willing to invest in it. He was so happy."

She passed me the plate of sweets and wasn't satisfied until I took a cookie. It was dense and buttery.

"They started to build the project—in the Westfjords. And then, just like that, the bubble burst. The economy collapsed. Baldur couldn't get the money he needed to finish the project. His investors had all gone broke. He couldn't repay his loan either, so he lost his fishing quota. We owed far more money than we could ever repay. Baldur was desperate, like so many people. But then a miracle happened, and he found some new investors. He thought everything was going to be okay. Then that woman came snooping around."

"You mean Gudrun?"

"Yes. She was a reporter for one of the newspapers. She started out doing recipes and articles about raising children, that kind of thing. But she was ambitious. The more her husband wanted her to stay home and look after Brynja, the more she wanted to do something important."

"Important?"

"That's what she used to say. She wanted to be the kind of reporter who breaks stories and grabs headlines. She got it into her head that Baldur was doing something wrong, and she started to follow him and pester him."

"What did she think he was doing?"

"She claimed that he was in league with criminals."

"What kind of criminals?"

"Russian criminals. She said that the people who invested in his project after the crash were financing it with money from drugs and human trafficking. She said they wanted to use the project, the casino especially, to launder money. She even claimed that they were going to use the place to transport drugs from here to other countries. Can you imagine anything so ridiculous? My Baldur would never get involved in anything like that."

"Did she have any proof?"

"Not that I know of. Not that the newspaper ever printed. Not that it even hinted at. Her editor said that he knew she was working on something, but that he hadn't assigned it to her and that she didn't want to say what it was until she had the whole story. You see what she was like? She wanted to make a big splash. She wanted to make a name for herself. Instead, she fell at Barnafoss."

"Barnafoss?"

"It's a waterfall not far from here. They found her in the water below. They say from the bruising, she either fell or jumped and then drowned. Then her husband started accusing my Baldur of murder."

Clearly Einar didn't think she fell or jumped.

"What did the police say?"

"They investigated and said that it was incon- clusive—that her death could have been accidental."

"Could have been?"

"The manner of death was ruled as *Undetermined*. She drowned, that's all."

"So why did Einar and Brynja think she was murdered?"

"Ah," she said. She sounded like my history teacher whenever someone asked an unexpectedly relevant question. "At first, they thought it was an accident too. But Einar couldn't figure out what she was doing at the top of the waterfall. How had she fallen in? He didn't know what she was working on either—not until Brynja came up with her crazy stories."

"Crazy stories?"

"Apparently she heard Gudrun talking to Baldur on several occasions. And it's true. Gudrun talked to him. Baldur never denied it. He said she was asking about the development and how it was going and whether it was true that some famous movie stars were thinking of buying some of the units—that kind of thing. She also found out that Baldur wasn't home that night. She said she knew her mother was working on a story about him and about the Russians he was working with. She's the one who started all the talk of murder."

We were sliding back into the Kingdom of Krazy.

"Why would she do that?"

"Because she was jealous. Because after Baldur sold his fishing quota, he bought my Rakel all the best clothes and all the latest gadgets. Gudrun didn't make a lot of money as a reporter, and her father is a tour guide. It's seasonal work at best. Brynja did it to get back at Rakel."

"Einar is convinced that your husband killed his wife because of something that Brynja said out of jealousy?"

Freyja looked deadly serious as she nodded. "She claims she heard her mother talking to someone before she left the house that night. She says her mother told whoever it was that she was going to confront Baldur with proof and that she was going to tape-record the conversation."

"What kind of proof?"

"I don't know. The police didn't find anything—no proof of anything, no tape recording, nothing like that."

I took a sip of coffee. I'm no Sherlock Holmes, but it sure sounded to me like Einar and Brynja had a case. They knew Gudrun was going to meet someone that night. They knew it had to do with the story she was working on. And they knew, because of what Brynja had heard, that Gudrun was going to try to get something incriminating out of Baldur. If I'd been playing ball with the Russian mob, or whatever, and someone was going to expose me, I know what I would have been tempted to do.

"Maybe she met someone there," Freyja said. "Maybe that person really did push her and that's why she died. But it wasn't Baldur. He would never do anything like that."

I hated to ask, but I had to. "Do you know where your husband was that night?"

She didn't try to avoid my eyes when she answered. "No. But when he came home late, everything was normal. I was married to him for nineteen years. Do you think I wouldn't know if my husband had killed someone? Do you think I wouldn't notice that something was wrong?"

I had no idea.

"Baldur was upset with all these accusations. Who wouldn't be? The police came several times to question him. People were talking. They said the most hateful things—how much he'd changed since he'd sold his quota, how he was throwing money around, how he liked to hobnob with wealthy foreigners. He was hurt and angry when he heard that. And he saw how upset Rakel was when she came home from school. Then he disappeared."

"What do you mean?"

"I mean, he called me one day to say that he would be late coming home because he had errands to run, and that was the last I heard of him."

"He didn't come home?"

"He didn't come home. He didn't call again. He disappeared. His car was found behind a warehouse down at the port."

"Did you contact the police?"

She nodded grimly. "They looked for him. They contacted all his friends and business associates. No one had heard from him since. They checked ships' manifests. They checked with the airlines. There was no record of him leaving the country."

"He just vanished into thin air?"

"The rumors started to fly again. It wouldn't surprise me if Einar started them. Everyone was saying that maybe it was true that Gudrun was on to something. Maybe Baldur was no better than a criminal, and maybe his criminal friends smuggled him out of the country on a boat. Other people, people I thought were my friends, said maybe he had decided to leave me for someone younger, one of the girls from the clubs where he used to meet the

Russians to do business. But Baldur wasn't like that. He was a good man. He just wanted something better for his family."

And now for the big question.

"What do you think happened to him, Freyja?"

"I think he's dead. I think Einar killed him."

ELEVEN

I didn't know what to say. I mean, what do you say when someone tells you that your host, the man your life was going to depend on in a few days, murdered someone?

I finished my coffee—fast. When she pressed me to talk to Einar and Brynja, I suggested she go to the police.

"The police!" She snorted. "Tryggvi knew my Baldur when they were boys. But he thinks I can't see the truth about him, that I'm crazy. They all do. But I'm not. I'm not." She got so worked up that she spilled her coffee.

I stood up and thanked her. I didn't know what else to say. I just knew I wanted to get out of there.

She followed me down the stairs, even though I told her she didn't have to bother and that I could see myself out. The whole time, she kept telling me that she wasn't crazy and that it was Einar who was the killer, not her husband. I was glad when I was finally out the door. And don't you know it, I had just stepped out onto the street when a familiar-looking suv slid by.

Einar.

He frowned at me as he sailed by.

I pulled away from Freyja's house with no destination in mind. Mostly I just wanted to put as much distance as possible between her and me. She could say she wasn't crazy until she was blue in the face, but that didn't make it so. I mean, if her husband had been murdered, the cops would know about it. They wouldn't treat her as if she was delusional. And, really, if old Baldur had been doing business with so-called Russian businessmen who were really Russian gangsters, well, call *me* crazy, but wasn't it far more likely that they were the ones who had bumped him off, not some

Icelandic tour guide? After all, according to Tryggvi, people didn't kill people in Iceland very often. I knew that handguns were illegal here. Icelandic cops didn't even carry them. And, anyway, look at the facts. Baldur had taken out a huge loan. Everything had gone bust—there'd been a massive economic meltdown that had started in the States and spread from there. Whole countries were going bankrupt. I have no idea what people do when they've lost everything. But I was willing to bet that some of them took a flier—ran from it all, put their miserable pasts behind them and made a fresh start somewhere else. Why was it so hard to believe that Baldur had done that?

I did a U-turn and headed back to the tourist information center. It was open but nearly deserted. The girl at the counter, who was gazing blankly out the window when I walked in, immediately brightened.

"How can I help you?" she asked. She was blond and blue-eyed, like most Icelanders I had met. She was also gorgeous, with a nice body and full pink lips. She looked about my age.

"I'd like directions to a place called Barnafoss,"

I said, stumbling over the word. I was pretty sure that was what Freyja had called it. "It's a waterfall. It's supposed to be somewhere near here."

The girl notched up her already bright smile.

"Where the children fell in and died," she said.

For a country with a supposedly low murder rate, an awful lot of people seemed to die terrible deaths.

"Barnafoss," she said sweetly. "It means Children's Waterfall. It got its name from two boys who lived at Hraunsas, a farm near there. One day their parents left the two boys at home while they went to church. But the boys had nothing to do, so they decided to follow their parents—"

I was guessing they must have been bored out of their skulls if the only thing they could think of to do was follow their parents to church. But that's just me.

"They took a shortcut," she said. "There used to be a stone bridge over the waterfall."

"Used to be?"

Her smile was dazzling.

"The boys got dizzy crossing the stone bridge. They fell into the water and drowned. When their mother found out what had happened, she put a spell on the bridge. A little while after that, there was an earthquake and the bridge collapsed." She reached under the counter and pulled out a map of the area. "It's a popular tourist attraction," she said. Whatever turns your crank, I guess. "Now…" She drew a red line on the map to show me how to get from the tourist center to the falls.

"It's easy to get to," she said. "It's very close."

"I heard a woman drowned there a year ago," I said.

"Yes, that's true."

"Does that happen often—people falling over the falls?"

"Hardly ever." She paused. "Although sometimes a tourist gets a little too close to the edge and slips, even though they are told to be careful. But as far as I know, none of them have drowned."

"What do you think happened to the woman who drowned?" I asked. "Did she get too close to the edge? Or do you think it had something to do with the spell that woman put on the bridge? Am I going to be in danger if I go up there?"

There was that megawatt smile again.

"If you are careful, you should be fine. The area is clearly marked and there are chains that keep people from going too close."

Chains? "Are they new?"

"New?"

"Did they put them up after that woman drowned?"

"No. They've been there for a long time."

"So what happened to her? Was she some crazy tourist who hopped over the chain to take a picture or something?" Yeah, I knew she wasn't. But I wanted to know what *she* knew.

"She was a reporter," the girl said. "She lived near here."

"Did she have some kind of medical condition? Did she faint or something?"

The girl leaned across the counter and dropped her voice, even though we were the only two people in the place.

"I heard she jumped."

"Suicide?"

"That's what I heard. She was having some troubles in her marriage, and she killed herself."

"Boy, I didn't hear that. Someone just mentioned that a woman had drowned. I thought it must have been an accident."

"It wasn't ruled an accident. They called it *Undetermined*. I heard that's because the family— the husband—talked the police and the coroner into ruling it that way because he wanted to spare the woman's grandfather the grief of knowing that his only granddaughter took her own life. It's a family that has had a lot of tragedies."

So I'd heard.

"At first the husband claimed that his wife had been murdered. It was quite a scandal around here. But I heard the police weren't able to find any evidence. That's why they ruled the death undetermined. The daughter was in my school. I didn't know her well—she was a year behind me."

"What does *she* think happened to her mother?"

"Murder." She shook her head. "She claimed her mother was murdered. She talked about it all the time. She even accused another girl's father of being the murderer. It was awful. In the end, she had some kind of breakdown and left school.

She hasn't gone back. The girl whose father she accused was so upset that she moved to Denmark."

"And what about you? What do you think happened?"

She shrugged. "Suicide. Definitely suicide. I'd kill myself if I was married to a man like Einar."

"Oh?"

She glanced around again and dropped her voice even lower.

"He wanted her to stay home all day and cook and clean. He didn't want her to work for that newspaper. Me—I have plans for my life. I'm going to study fashion design. I'm going to have a career. I'm not going to stay in this miserable country for the rest of my life, and I'm certainly not going to dedicate my life to cooking and cleaning for a man—especially not a tour guide."

I picked up the map.

"Thanks for your help," I said.

"Don't cross the chain markers and you'll be fine." She flashed me another smile. "My name is Jonina, by the way." She made it sound like the prettiest name in the world. "I get off at seven this evening. In case you decide you want something a little more exciting to do."

I thanked her again. She really was a knockout. She could have been a model, never mind fashion designer.

Jonina was right. Barnafoss wasn't far. When I got there, a bunch of tourists were trekking from it to their tour bus. The only vehicle around was a Jeep with a pretty girl at the wheel talking into a cell phone. I got out of the car and started for the falls. There was a clear path and guide chains everywhere, presumably to keep tourists away from the edge of the falls and the river.

I stopped at a large display board to read about the falls—it said pretty much what Jonina had told me. The trail branched in a couple of directions to allow different vantage points of the falls. I followed the one that led to the highest point. The terrain was rocky—all terrain in Iceland seemed to be rocky, but when I got up high enough, it changed from rough footing to enormous swirls, as if someone had poured liquid rock all over the ground and it had suddenly cooled. I'd never seen anything like it.

I kept climbing, looking down at the rock all the way. When I got to where the chain was at the top, I stepped over it and kept going, drawn now by the head of the falls. I think that's why I didn't notice the figure at the very top, right near the edge of the rock overlooking the water, until it was too late.

She rose from where she had been sitting behind some scrubby growth.

"What are you doing here?" she demanded.

I almost fell backward when she jumped up like that.

"Jeez, you scared me," I said.

"What are you doing here?"

Great. She was in one of those moods again—queen of the world taking her problems out on the lowly peasant boy.

"Seeing the sights," I said. "Jonina at the tourist information center told me this place has quite a history. She gave me this." I held up the map.

"Jonina!" Brynja snorted. "Is that *all* she gave you?"

Meow!

"What about you? What are you doing up here when your friend is waiting down there for you?" I asked.

"Johanna understands," she said.

She sank back down and sat cross-legged on a huge swirl of rock and stared out over the raging torrent below. I looked down. It was a long drop into the water that swept almost immediately through several narrow, rocky channels before falling again over another enormous lip of rock. Freyja had said the body was bruised. If Gudrun had fallen from up here—or if she had jumped or been pushed—her body must have been more than bruised; it must have been battered.

"Aren't you freezing sitting on that rock?" I asked.

Brynja looked up at me in annoyance.

"Are you still here?" she said in a tone calculated to drive any normal person away. Too bad for her, I'm not a normal person. I have a pig head. At least, that's how the Major puts it. His English is terrific— except for some of the more idiomatic expressions. He doesn't cover all the bases; he covers them *up*. For him, things sell like pancakes, not hotcakes. You get the idea.

I sat down beside her. She moved sideways away from me.

"Are you okay?" I asked.

"I'm fine." Snarl, snap.

"You don't seem fine. You look kinda…sad." Yeah, that was it. "You look sad."

She scowled at me. Okay, at that exact second she didn't look sad. She looked good and angry.

"We don't have to be enemies, Brynja."

"We don't have to be friends either. You're going with my dad in a few days to do whatever it is you came here to do. And then you're leaving."

"So?"

"So you're just another tourist. They come and they go. You're not part of my life."

"I still care if you're upset." At least, I sort of did.

"It's nothing." But her voice was softer now and she was staring into the water below.

I kept my mouth shut, looked around and wondered what had brought Brynja's mother up here of all places. Was it like Jonina had said? Had she come up here intending to end her life? Had she jumped? Or was there some other reason she had come here? Did this place have anything to do with Freyja's missing husband? Had she come up here to meet him? But why *here*? I glanced at Brynja. I knew what she was doing here, and, even though she might not have believed it, I understood why she wanted to be alone. I stood up.

"I guess I'll see you later," I said.

She looked at me but didn't say anything.

I turned to go back down the way I had come.

"Do you think about your mother?" she asked just as I was about to step over the chain marker.

I looked back at her.

"You said she died," she said. "Do you think about her much?"

Did I think about her *much*? Was she kidding?

"I think about her all the time." All I had to do was close my eyes, and there she was, her long brown hair, her sparking eyes, her smile, always a smile. And then, sometimes, more times than I could stand at first but lately less and less, I see that gigantic rock smashing one whole side of the car. Her side. That rock where my mother should have been. Where she was.

"Rennie?"

I had to force myself to focus on her.

"How did she die?"

"Car accident." I don't know why I always said it that way, like another car had crashed into hers or she had crashed into someone else's car. But it was better than saying rock accident. If you said car accident, most people got a picture in their minds and just left it at that. Everyone could understand the idea. But rock accident? You had to explain that. What rock? Where had it come from? Where did it land? When you explained all that, you had to live it all over again. And when you did that—when I did that— I had to face the fact that it was all my fault. I'd driven her crazy that whole trip. No matter what she'd done, I'd wanted more. If only...

"It was a car accident."

"How did you find out?"

"Huh?" What was she talking about? How did I find out about what?

"I was at school," she said. "Geography class. I like geography. I'm good at it. I like it. I was thinking perhaps I would be a geologist. Iceland is a paradise for geologists, did you know that?" She didn't wait for an answer. "It's over a rift zone where two tectonic plates meet. It's also over a hot spot, which accounts for all the volcanoes. It's one of the newest islands on earth, geologically speaking— Iceland is twenty to twenty-five million years old."

That sounded pretty old to me. "I was in class. The teacher was handing back test papers, and I looked up and I saw my father and the school director outside the classroom door. I remember wondering what my father was doing there. Then the director gestured to my teacher and she went outside and he said something to her. When she came back in, she called my name and said I was wanted out in the hall. I remember she closed the door after I left the room. I couldn't think why she did that. She always left the door open. Then my father told me. I didn't believe him, of course. I screamed at him. I called him a liar, over and over. I guess that's why my teacher closed the door. I guess she knew I'd be upset."

"Anyone would be if they got the news that their mother had jumped or been pushed or whatever over a waterfall."

Her eyes hardened. She stood up.

"Who said she jumped over the waterfall?"

"Or was pushed," I said. Jeez, she looked like she was going to push *me* over. "Or whatever."

"It was Jonina, wasn't it?" She shoved me in the chest, which I wasn't expecting. It threw me off balance.

"You talked to Jonina about my mother, and she told you that my mother jumped, didn't she? Didn't she?" She shoved me again, harder this time, and even though I saw it coming, I stumbled and my foot slipped close to the edge of the rock.

"Hey, Brynja, take it easy," I said.

"She didn't jump! I don't care what she told you. I don't care what anyone told you. My mother didn't jump. Someone pushed her."

"Okay," I said. I kept my voice calm and quiet. "Okay." I was holding my hands up in front of me to block her if she decided to push me again. "I'm sorry. I didn't mean to upset you."

She was glowering at me, and for a moment I thought she was going to lash out again. Then her hands fell to her sides.

"Just go away and leave me alone," she said.

Tears pooled in her eyes. Her shoulders slumped, and I couldn't remember when I had seen anyone look so—what was the word?—stricken. No, that's not quite right. I remember the look on the Major's face when he showed up at the hospital where I'd been taken. I wasn't hurt, not really. My fingernails were ripped and the ends of my fingers were bleeding

142

from trying to lift a rock that refused to budge. My head ached from the impact with the air bag. And my muscles screamed at me, every single one of them, from the exertion I had subjected them to. But, really, none of it amounted to what you would call a real injury. Mostly I'd been taken there because I was in shock. And because they wanted to take some X-rays, just in case. Then the Major had showed up, just like Brynja's father had. He was the one who made it official, who told me what I had been refusing to believe. Brynja looked like that now.

"Look, Brynja—"

"Just go." She turned away from me and raised a hand to wipe away tears that she didn't want me to see.

I hung there for a moment. If I left her, what would she do? I remembered all the times I had thought about my mom and how she had lost her life to a rock that had missed me by no more than a couple of inches. Maybe not even that much. Somehow that rock had skimmed over the top of my head and come crashing down right into the driver's seat. My mom's seat. I thought about it all the time. I thought about it on the anniversaries of when it happened.

I thought about it on my mother's birthday and at Christmas. I thought about it at Thanksgiving and Mother's Day. It came to me in dreams and nightmares. It changed everything—and I do mean everything—for me and for the Major.

But I'm still here.

I'm dealing with it. At least, I think I am—most days.

I picked my way back down the rocky hill and along the path to my car. When I got to the parking area, I interrupted Johanna's call and told her that Brynja needed her. I looked back just once, as I was turning the key in the ignition. Brynja was standing exactly where I had left her. She hadn't moved at all.

TWELVE

I took my time driving back to the house. Einar's suv wasn't in the driveway when I got there. I let myself in. Someone called from the back of the house and then appeared in the hall between the kitchen and the front door. Elin.

"He's been asking for you," she said. "Please, come."

I joined her at the back of the house, where she stood aside to let me go into the old man's bedroom. He was propped up against some pillows, his cheeks almost as white as the snowy linen.

"David," he said.

I glanced at Elin.

"Go ahead," she said. "He's been asking for you all afternoon. He says he has something to tell you."

"But I'm not—"

"Don't be afraid," she said, smiling encouragingly at me. "He won't bite."

"David," the old man said again.

I went in and sat down on the chair beside his bed.

"I'll leave you two alone," Elin said. "If you need me for anything, just shout." She disappeared from sight.

I leaned closer so that the old man could see me clearly.

"It's not David," I said. "It's Rennie. I'm Rennie."

He said something in Icelandic. At least, I think it was Icelandic.

"Are you okay, Mister…Sigurdur?" I asked.

"Too many secrets," he said. "They're a burden to the soul."

"Mister, uh, sir—"

"I want to tell you something before it's too late."

Too late? What was he talking about?

"It's out there," he said. He raised one thin hand off the quilt and pointed to the window. "I saw it. I knew what it was, and I rejoiced. I am ashamed but I rejoiced, even though I knew it was wrong. Help me."

At first I didn't understand. Then I saw he was trying to get out of bed.

"Help me."

"I don't think that's a good idea, sir."

His face was red from his struggle to lift himself up off his pillows.

"Sir, I—"

"Help me. I want to show you." He had got himself almost to a sitting position and was easing his feet toward the edge of the bed.

"Elin!" I shouted.

The old man's thin legs poked out from under the covers and slipped to the floor. He tried to push himself up off the bed.

"Elin!" I shouted again.

He struggled to his feet.

"I want to show you." He was tottering to the window, pointing again, and I was sure he was going to fall over. I threw my arms around him to hold him up.

A deep voice barked something in Icelandic.

Einar.

"What the devil do you think you're doing?" he shouted. At me.

"He got out of bed," I said. "I tried to stop him."

Einar flew across the room, shoved me aside and took hold of the old man. Elin rushed into the room.

"Einar!" She ran to the bedside. "What are you doing?"

"He got up," I said again, but no one listened to me. Einar and Elin got the old man back into bed and covered him up. He was breathing hard. Elin grabbed his wrist to take his pulse. The whole time she was doing that, Einar was yelling at her. Based on my experience with the Major, I'd say he was reaming her out for leaving him alone with me. They argued with each other in Icelandic until, finally, Einar stormed out of the room. I found him pacing angrily up and down in the living room.

"It wasn't her fault," I said.

"She's paid to look after him."

"She *was* looking after him. She was with him when I got back. He wanted to talk to me."

"What on earth about?"

"I don't know. He thought I was my grandfather. He kept calling me David."

Einar stared at me as if I were out of my mind.

"He has a photo," I said. "From just after my grandfather crash-landed here during the war. He thinks I look like him."

"What did he want to talk to you about?"

"I don't know. He decided to get out of bed and that's when I called for Elin. Then you showed up."

He was calming down. I guess seeing the old man out of bed had given him a scare, but he nodded now and apologized for yelling at me. I told him I understood.

"I'm going to call his doctor," he said. "And then I should get dinner started."

When I offered to help, he shook his head.

"You're still a guest here, and my guests don't have to make their own meals. Besides, I like to cook. It calms me."

I didn't know what else to do, so I browsed through the bookshelves in the living room, found a novel in English that looked like it might be okay, and took it outside to sit and read. From where I was, at the side of the house, I could see the old man's window. I sure hoped he was okay. I wondered what he'd been talking about. What secrets did he mean? What had he known was wrong, and what did he mean he'd been happy about it? What had he been planning to show me?

I looked at the window and with my eye traced a path from it, trying to figure out what he had been pointing at. It could have been almost anything. From his window, the land rolled until it hit the sea. First there was the yard, then fields, then a stream, then more fields and, far, far in the distance just where the land curved, another farm. I opened the book and started to read. The story was okay, but not exactly gripping. I looked up again. This time I got up and walked back to the old man's window. Elin must have drawn the shades because they were down now. I turned so that my back was to them and took another look. He'd wanted to show me something. It had been important enough to him that he'd got himself out of bed, which, from the way everyone had reacted, not only was not good for him but was also something he hadn't done in a long time. And all because there was something he wanted to show me—or my grandfather.

Yard. Fence. Fields. Stream. Fields. Distant farm.

Distant farm? Who did it belong to? Had something happened over there? Had he seen something? What?

Yard. Fence. Fields. Stream…

Wait a minute, what was that hump of land out in the yard? It looked like a hill. I started to walk toward it, the whole time telling myself I was being ridiculous. The old man was clearly delusional; he'd already mistaken me for my grandfather.

I almost turned back, when I saw that the little hill wasn't a hill after all. I circled around it. It was a shed or a little house that had been built into the rock and was covered with grass, as if the land had grown over it. It had a sturdy double door made of thick planks. As I was walking toward it, I heard a car door slam. Brynja was back.

She climbed out of Johanna's car, waved goodbye and then stood for a moment on the driveway staring at me. When Einar appeared at the door, Brynja pointed to me. Einar came down the front steps and started toward me. Brynja trotted along behind him, a quizzical look on her face. I headed back to meet them.

"How is he?" I asked.

"How is who?" asked Brynja.

"Your afi," I said. "He wasn't feeling well."

Brynja turned to her father, who assured her

that everything was under control. The doctor was coming to see him this evening.

"But what happened?" Brynja asked, a note of panic in her voice.

"He was feeling ill," Einar said.

"He didn't recognize me," I put in. "He thought I was my grandfather."

Brynja said something in Icelandic to her father. She sounded upset. He put an arm around her, and his response had a soothing tone to it.

"Let's all go back into the house and have dinner," Einar said. "Brynja, you can set the table."

She jogged on ahead. My guess: she was going to see her grandfather and the table could take care of itself.

"I'm sure this isn't what you bargained for when you came over here," Einar said. "All this family drama."

"Stuff happens," I said. "It's no one's fault."

He smiled, but there was a weariness behind it. "So I noticed you discovered a bit of our history."

Huh?

"The turf hut," he said, nodding at the grass-covered structure. "It's what people used to live in, in the old days. With trees so scarce—well, virtually nonexistent—the old-timers built their homes out of rocks and turf, very much like some of your settlers used to build sod houses. The only difference is that your sod houses were very temporary. People lived in them only for as long as it took to build something more substantial. But here, people lived in turf huts for generations."

"Someone actually lived in that?" I said, staring in wonder at the small structure.

"In that particular hut, no," Einar said. "It's been a storage shed for as long as I can remember. It's filled with junk—stuff from the old days. I don't think anyone has been in there in years." He nodded toward the house. "Come on. Let's go and have dinner."

I followed him into the house, but as I walked across the lawn, I couldn't stop thinking about the old man and what it was that he'd wanted to show me. He had pointed in the direction of the turf hut. It was the only structure between here and the horizon, which meant it was the only thing he could have been pointing at besides the stream or the distant farmhouse in the meadow. But what secret could an old turf hut be hiding? Einar said that it had old stuff in it and that no one ever went inside.

Had the old man stashed something in there? Was it something to do with the woman whose face filled the pages of my grandfather's journal? The old man didn't want me to show it to Einar or Brynja. He didn't want me to tell them anything about it. But he wanted to show me—well, my grandfather— something. Something he had seen that was wrong. It had to be something about the woman. If so, what? I wondered. Boy, did I wonder.

The meal that night reminded me of dinner at my place after my mother died. On the nights when the Major didn't make it home until late or when he was on assignment somewhere, he left me in the haphazard care of Mrs. Fernie, the woman who came in several times a week to clean and, when I was younger, to make sure I did my homework. She cooked, too, and, when the Major couldn't be there, stayed over, sleeping on a pull-out couch in the den. I liked Mrs. Fernie, even though she was a terrible cook. She had a boys-will-be-boys attitude to supervising me and never minded if I wanted to horse around with my friends or stay out later than my nine o'clock curfew, which she regarded as overly restrictive. The Major though—he was another story.

When it was just the Major and me, dinner was a dismal affair. The meal was always perfectly balanced and excruciatingly nutritional. We had our protein, our carbs and our veggies. Lots of veggies. Stuff like broccoli, spinach, kale, Brussels sprouts. Fried foods were out. Sugar—forget about it. A meal for the Major wasn't about the food. It was about fuel designed to power a soldier. And it was consumed to the rhythm of the Major's knife and fork chinking against the dinner plate at precise bite-chew intervals, punctuated by an occasional irritated "Eat it before it gets cold, Rennie." The Major never talked about his day—everything he did was cloaked in confidentiality—and I sure didn't talk about mine. Anything fun I did he would have disapproved of, and anything bad I did, any trouble I got into, he'd hear about soon enough without me having to confess. I couldn't wait until he'd set down his knife and fork and tell me to clear the table and wash the dishes, which he did every night, even though I did exactly that, every night. I used to wish the words would appear above his head in a cartoon balloon, so that I could grab them and ram them down his throat.

The meal in Einar's kitchen that night wasn't much better. Sure, the food was different—grilled fish, boiled potatoes and mushy canned peas. The faces around the table were different. Brynja kept looking anxiously through the door at her grandfather and, if her eyes accidentally met mine, made it clear that she wished I wasn't there. Einar, like the Major, ate in silence until, I guess, he remembered I was there. Then he asked how I had amused myself all day. When I said I'd just been sightseeing, Brynja scowled at me. Einar didn't notice. The meal broke up when the doorbell rang. Brynja raced to answer. It was the doctor. Einar and Brynja followed him into the old man's room. I made myself useful clearing the table and doing the dishes, just like at home.

I was in the living room, the same less-than-gripping novel in my hand while I stared out at the back of the turf shed, when the doctor came through with Einar. They were talking in Icelandic, but their somber voices told me that things were not well with the old man. After Einar showed the doctor out, he turned to me and said that our trip would be delayed by a couple of days.

"My father-in-law needs to go to the hospital for some tests," he said. "He'll be transported there tomorrow. I'd like to see how that goes before I take you out. I hope you don't mind."

"If you want, I mean, considering the circumstances, I could find someone else to take me."

Einar shook his head.

"I signed on to do this. It means a lot to Sigurdur that you're here. He thought highly of your grandfather. I'd like to do the job if I can."

I nodded, but really I wished he would pass the assignment on to someone else. What did it matter who took me to the interior so long as I did what my grandfather had asked me to do? And the sooner I did that, the sooner I could say goodbye to Brynja and her attitude.

"Let me see how things are after we get the test results," Einar said. "Fair enough?"

"Fair enough," I said.

I couldn't get to sleep. I kept thinking about the old man, the journal with its sketches, and what the old man had wanted to show me. About my grand-father, too, and his journal, and the letter he'd left for me. In it, he'd written that he'd always suspected that Sigurdur knew something about the woman who had saved him, but that he was uncomfortable when the subject was raised. But now, here Sigurdur was talking about something bad that had happened. Talking about too many secrets too. He wanted to get at least one of them off his chest. He wanted to tell the one person he thought he could trust. The only trouble was, that person was dead.

I didn't know about my grandfather David McLean until after my mother died. It happened one night, maybe two weeks after the funeral, after all Mom's friends had stopped coming over all the time with food, after the whirl of decisions to be made about the funeral and the service and the burial site, after the Major's relatives (who had adored my mother) had all returned to Quebec, and after Grandma Mel, as stricken as the Major, had boarded a plane and flown back to Vancouver. It was a quiet night, with not a sound in the house because the Major forbade television on school nights and didn't think a person could study with the radio on and had refused to get me the iPod I'd asked for at least a dozen times. I was sitting at the dining-room table staring blankly at my history book. He was in the living room, reading some reports. And the phone rang.

I answered.

I could tell by the voice at the other end that the caller was an old man. He wanted to know if he had reached the residence of Major André Charbonneau. The husband of Suzanne Timson Charbonneau. I had never heard my mother referred to that way, but Grandma Mel's last name was Timson, so I said yes. Then he wanted to know to whom he had the pleasure of speaking.

I was just about to tell him to buzz off—I figured him for some kind of salesman—when the Major grabbed the phone from me and told me to get back to work.

My pleasure.

The Major talked—well, mostly listened—for a few minutes. He said he couldn't make any promises. He said he had to absorb what he'd just been told. He hung up the phone and sat down on the sofa again but didn't pick up his newspaper.

"Who was it?" I asked.

"He says he's your grandfather."

I laughed. "Pull the other one. I know *Grandpère*'s voice when I hear it." One big clue: Grandpère Pierre always spoke French.

"He says he's your mother's father," the Major said. He got up again, picked up the phone and dialed. A moment later I heard him say, "Mel?"

Secrets.

Secrets come out sooner or later. Like when Grandma Mel flew back a few weeks later to talk to the Major and me in person about when she was young and working in an art gallery while she finished her dissertation. In came a handsome (according to her) young (according to her) widower with four daughters and a keen interest in art. They chatted. They clicked. He invited her for coffee, which turned into the longest cup of coffee she ever had. They fell in love. Deeply in love. He started to talk about marriage. Then she got a job offer—in France. He didn't want to move his daughters so far away when their lives were so settled. Besides, he told her, there were plenty of job opportunities here.

"I hadn't even met the daughters yet," Grandma Mel said. "Frankly, the notion scared me. It wouldn't be just David and me. It would be David and me and four girls, some of them already young women. I took the job and that was the end of it."

Except for one small thing that turned out to be my mother.

"I never told him," Grandma Mel said. "It would just have complicated things."

It did anyway, because the death notice that the Major had placed in the national newspaper had given my mother's age and named her mother. David McLean had seen it. He'd figured it out. And now I had a grandfather—one who wanted to make the acquaintance of the grandson he never knew he had, the son of the daughter he never knew he had until it was too late.

"Sorry, Grandma Mel," I said. "Not interested."

"Sorry, Melanie," the Major said. "If the boy isn't interested, *que'est-ce que je peux faire?* What can I do?"

End of story?

No way.

I started getting into trouble. It was small stuff at first—skipping school, blowing off homework, smart-mouthing teachers. From there it went to explosions of rage, mostly taken out in fights with other guys, which I usually got suspended for. That only gave me more time to get into trouble. I started breaking into people's houses—I don't even know why. I did it maybe half a dozen times before I got caught. The Major blew a gasket. And I ran. Where to? To the grandfather I never knew I had and who—let's face it—I'd been curious about.

It turned out I liked my grandfather a lot. He was superold, his body was slow, but his mind was as sharp as a tack. I hung out with him for a month before the Major came and dragged me back to, as he put it, "meet the music." And that's how I ended up with Worm, Boot, Capone, Jimi and good old Gerard.

I thumbed through the journal again and made a second attempt to read the faded letter tucked into it. I glanced at my watch and wondered if it was too late to make a phone call. I dug out the phone number the Major had given me and made it anyway.

I awoke to voices and commotion. I pulled on my jeans, grabbed a sweatshirt and went to the top of the stairs. The old man was being carried out of the house on a stretcher. I put on my sweatshirt and went downstairs. Brynja and Einar followed the stretcher and watched as two attendants slid it into an ambulance. Einar climbed into his suv.

Brynja said something to him. They argued until Einar spotted me.

"Brynja, we went over this last night," he said in exasperated English. "You can't do anything. I'm just going to be sitting around waiting for him while they do tests. And someone has to take care of our guest. Make a lunch and take a hike along the stream. Show him around. And stop worrying. I'll call you as soon as I know anything."

Brynja glared at me.

"He's *your* client, not *my* guest," she said.

"I can take care of myself," I said for what seemed like the zillionth time. I had plans that definitely did not include Brynja.

"I'm going with you," Brynja said.

"You are not." Einar Sounded exasperated.

The ambulance attendants closed and secured the door and drove off. Einar climbed into his suv and took off after them.

Brynja watched until he was out of sight. She held out her hand.

"Keys," she said.

"Excuse me?"

"Give me the keys to the car. I want to go to the hospital."

"Your dad said you're supposed to stay here."

"I bet you always do what your father tells you," she said, a knowing smirk on her face, like she had me all figured out. Nothing bugs me more than people who think they know me when, in fact, they know nothing at all about me.

"Where I come from, we say please."

Her hand remained extended. She did not say please.

"You said you could look after yourself," she said. "So do it."

"Good idea. See you later." I headed for the Yaris and slid into the driver's seat.

Brynja jumped in beside me before I could lock her out.

"Where are you going?" she demanded.

"Reykjavik," I said, "not that it's any of your business."

"What for?"

"To meet someone. A friend of my dad's."

"Good. You can drop me at the hospital." She buckled her seat belt and waited for me to start the car.

"Fine," I said. "But you have to promise not to tell your dad. Tell him you hitchhiked or something."

"He'd kill me if he thought I did that."

"So tell him one of your friends took you."

She thought it over. A faint smile appeared on her face.

"Let's go," she said.

THIRTEEN

Brynja complained that I drove too slowly and wasn't nearly aggressive enough passing the cars ahead of me. In response, I slowed down even more and refused to pass anything. Brynja fumed in the passenger seat next to me, but there was nothing she could do.

When we finally reached Reykjavik, she gave me directions to the hospital. I was glad when I could finally pull over and let her out.

"Do you want me to pick you up later?" I asked.

"No, I'll go back with my dad."

She slammed the door. Fine with me.

I drove around until I found one of the tourist information centers that seemed to dot the country. I parked my car, waited in line until a Jonina look-alike finished with a German tourist, and asked for directions to the nearest newspaper office. It turned out to be a twenty-minute walk. I left my car where it was and set off on foot.

Reykjavik—or at least the part of it I was in—was a densely inhabited city. There were no huge high-rises or skyscrapers. But neither were there huge yards. Most of the houses I passed opened right onto the sidewalk, and they were all jammed together. If they had yards, they were hidden in the back somewhere. A lot of their exteriors were brightly colored corrugated iron—green, red, dark blue, yellow—that was supposed to stand up well to the corrosive salt air.

The main thing I noticed as I strolled through the city was the quiet. There were cars on the street, but unlike every other city I had ever visited, there was no underlying roar of traffic. There were people on the street too, but there was no aural wallpaper of voices. There were also no sirens, no rumbling buses, no screaming kids, no dogs barking—in fact, very few dogs at all. There were a lot of cats though. And because most buildings were no more than stories high, it was easy to locate the taller newspaper building. Once I'd sighted it, all I had to do was keep walking toward it.

I told the receptionist I had an appointment with Geir. She picked up a phone and spoke to someone. Eventually a man appeared. He smiled, shook my hand and asked how his nephew Jakob was.

"He's doing great," I said.

"Is he married yet?"

Married? Jake? That would be the day! I shook my head, and Jake's uncle sighed.

"Well, what can I do for you?" he asked.

"I'm trying to find out about a woman." He waited expectantly for details, but I didn't know what else to say except, "She had something to do with rescuing my grandfather." I told him about the plane crash back during the war, and he nodded.

"I heard about that it was big news. The Americans at the base sent out a search party. There was only one survivor. That was your grandfather?"

I nodded.

He glanced at the receptionist and then led me through a doorway and into what looked like a conference room. We sat.

"This woman you mentioned," he said. "You say she saved your grandfather?"

"He seemed to think so."

Geir frowned. "I don't remember hearing anything about that. My father was a reporter. He never mentioned a woman."

I told him about the letter my grandfather had written and the journal he had left me. "I want to find out who she was," I said. "But I'm not sure how to go about it."

"Well, I suppose the place to start is the news-paper from that time."

"Can I go through them?"

He smiled. "Do you read Icelandic?" When I shook my head, he said, "I suppose I can look for you. What do you know about her?"

"Not much." In fact, almost nothing. I pulled journal from my pocket and showed it to him. "She looked like this."

He studied her face. "I suppose that's a start," he said. "You'll have to give me a little time. Can you give me a phone number where I can reach you?"

I gave him my cell number.

"May I make a copy of one of these sketches?"

I nodded. He disappeared for a moment and then returned with the journal and a copy of one of the pages.

"I'll let you know if I find anything." He started to guide me to the door again.

"Um, Mr. Geir…"

"Just Geir. We don't use last names the way you Canadians do."

"Right. I was wondering, did you know a reporter named Gudrun?"

"Gudrun Njalsdottir?"

No last names, but second names.

"Yeah."

"I worked rather closely with her. May I know why you ask?"

I shrugged. What was I supposed to say— I'm asking because I'm nosy?

"I heard about her—that she jumped off a water- fall, that she fell accidentally, that she was pushed."

Name a version and I'd heard it. It was true—that's what I heard. "I was wondering which it was."

He sighed. "I believe the police finally settled on *Undetermined*." He peered at me again. "And you ask because—?"

"Because Gudrun's grandfather and my grandfather were friends."

He smiled. "Your grandfather, the Canadian Air Force pilot."

"Yes."

"How is Sigurdur?"

"He's in the hospital for tests. I think his family is worried about him."

"I'm sorry to hear it. Yes, I knew Gudrun very well. As I said, I worked closely with her."

"And what do you think happened to her? Do you think she jumped?"

He peered at me. "Frankly? No. I know what people said. And I knew that Einar wasn't happy about her working, especially when she left the women's pages of the newspaper and started to do regular reporting. The hours were unpredictable. She wasn't always home when he wanted her there. Gudrun lacked confidence when she started working here.

She was so timid, afraid to ask questions. I used to say that she was like a beautiful flower without fertilizer. The work was the fertilizer. It made her bloom. She thrived on it. And then she wanted more. She wanted bigger stories, meatier stories. Something that she hoped would prove to the bosses that she could handle the tough stuff."

"Like the story she was researching when she died?" I said.

"Ah. Baldur and the Russians."

"You know about it?" Freyja told me that the newspaper's editor had denied any knowledge of what she'd been working on.

"I found out after she died," Geir said. "Einar told me. He knew about the story. I think he was the only person who did. Like I said, she was keeping it to herself until she broke it. She worked that story day and night, researching the Russians—well, as best as one could. It's not that easy to get information on what goes on in that country. But she was dogged. Is that the right word? Dogged?"

"Determined, you mean?"

"Very determined. She had half a dozen notebooks filled with notes. She never left them at the office, she was so paranoid."

"Paranoid?"

"She didn't want anyone here finding out what she was doing. I think she was afraid someone more experienced would take the story away from her. She wrote her notes in French."

He must have seen the puzzled look on my face.

"A lot of Icelanders speak more than one language besides Icelandic. Most speak Danish because of the historic link with Denmark and because many were educated at universities in Denmark. And a lot of people speak English these days as well. Then maybe some German or some other language. Gudrun was fluent in French. When she wanted to make sure that no one was looking over her shoulder, she wrote in French. I think she was also worried that the Russians had informers, but I don't know how realistic that was."

"So you don't know what she wrote?"

"I don't know French."

"I do," I said.

He looked interested.

"These notebooks she had—did the police look at them?"

"The whole half-dozen," he said. "I handed them over myself. But they must not have found anything helpful because nothing came of it. And there was nothing that showed that she had been pushed—or that she'd jumped for that matter. The place where she died, it's all water and rock."

"I've been there."

"Then you know. Her car was found nearby, but there were no other tire tracks that they were able to find. No fingerprints. No trace that anyone else had been there with her that night."

"There's not much around there," I said. What an understatement. There was nothing at all around there. "What do you think she was doing at those falls in the middle of the night?"

"That's where the suicide theory comes in," Geir said. "What indeed would she have been doing there? She might have gone there to meet someone, but that was never proved. Or she might have gone there for some other reason."

"Like, to jump. Or to look at the falls and then slip."

"You sound as convinced as I am," he said with a wry smile.

"What do you think happened?" I asked.

"Her family thinks she was murdered. They think she went there to meet Baldur and that he pushed her over the falls to stop her from writing her story."

"I heard he wasn't home that night."

Geir gave me an odd look. "You know quite a lot about the story."

"Like I said, my grandfather and her grandfather were friends."

"Baldur was not home that night. He says he was down by the ocean, thinking. It's well known that he often went down to the water to think. No one saw him, of course. But, again, there was nothing at all to tie him to Barnafoss, and the police didn't turn up anything in Gudrun's notes that would have given him a motive to kill her."

"But you think he did it?"

"I think someone did. The likely person is Baldur. If Gudrun was right about him, he certainly had a motive. He had no alibi. The police had him in custody for a while. It's just his luck that they couldn't prove he had anything to do with what happened that night. They had to let him go."

"Maybe they didn't know what they were doing. With so few murders here, they can't have much homicide experience." Tryggvi had told me that.

"The officer in charge, an Andersson, I think, was trained in America."

"Was he trained by the FBI?" I asked.

Geir nodded. "That sounds right. He seemed to know what he was doing."

Right, to distinguish him from all the other cops named Tryggvi. I didn't get it. These Icelanders kept saying they didn't have last names like the rest of the world, but when you asked about someone, the way I'd asked Tryggvi about Gudrun, they used a second name to make sure I understood who they were talking about. It was nuts.

"What about the fact that Baldur disappeared almost immediately. Didn't that make anyone suspicious?"

"It made *me* suspicious," he said. "It made Einar suspicious. Sigurdur too. No one knows where Baldur went. No one has heard from him. Not even his wife."

"She thinks he's dead."

"She may be right."

"She thinks Einar killed him."

"I know. She used to call me all the time to get me to work on a story about him. But Einar was at home that night. Sigurdur took an oath. If you ask me, it's the Russians who are responsible. They don't like people poking their noses into their affairs. And they don't like business partners who give people an excuse to poke around in their affairs."

"What happened to the project they were investing in with Baldur?" I asked.

"It stopped for a while. But I hear it's gearing up again. Somehow, don't ask me how, the Russians have money to invest when no one else does. You can only imagine where it came from." He glanced at his watch. "You must excuse me. If I find out anything about your mystery woman, I will call you. If there's anything else—"

"Yeah. You can tell me why names here are so messed up. How can you tell who belongs to what family?" It would never have occurred to me that Gudrun Njalsdottir was married to Einar Magnusson and that their daughter was Brynja Einarsdottir.

He laughed. "It takes getting used to, I'm sure. Both ways." When I looked puzzled, he said, "People who move here have to get used to it. So do people who move away—they have to adopt a new name system too."

"An easier one," I said.

He raised an eyebrow. Not all women in North America change their names to their husbands' when they marry. Sometimes they use two names."

He had a point. But my mom hadn't been one of those women—because the Major wasn't the kind of guy to entertain such a notion.

I thanked him and left.

I walked back to my car and sat behind the wheel trying to decide what to do next. I could head back to the house and take a closer look at that turf hut. Or—I glanced at my watch; it was still early—I could drop by the hospital and see what was what with the old man. There was no chance that Brynja was going to want to come back with me. She had already made that clear. On the other hand, there was every chance that Einar would ask me to take her home.

I decided to head back to the house. Alone.

I pulled out of my parking spot and retraced my route out of the city. I'm good at navigating. I have a good memory. The Major knows it too, which is one of the (many) things about me that drive him crazy. He's always at me with, "Why is it that you can remember every engine part and exactly where it goes or all the words to those god-awful songs you listen to, but you can't remember who won the War of 1812 or how to find the circumference of a circle?" Quick answer: because some things matter and some things don't. Care to guess which is which?

I parked my car and headed across the lawn to the turf hut.

As I reached out to pull open the solid wooden door, I noticed that an arc of ground in front of it had been scraped clean of grass from the door being opened and closed. I tugged on the door. It didn't give. I thought it must be secured in some way, but I didn't see a lock. I pulled again, harder this time. It opened.

I slipped inside.

The hut seemed even smaller inside than it had looked from the outside. It was no more than 8 feet wide and maybe 10 feet deep. The ceiling was low; there wasn't enough headroom for me to stand up straight. There was no light inside, either, other than what came in through the door. But this had to be where the old man was pointing. There was something in here that he wanted to show me, and judging from what he had said and the fact that he'd called me by my grandfather's name, it had to have something to do with my grandfather and the woman in his journal. The old man knew who she was. He'd been stunned to see her face. He desperately wanted me to keep it secret from Brynja and her father. He knew about something bad that had happened, and he'd wanted to tell my grandfather—maybe because he thought it was his last chance.

Old tools and implements—farm implements of some kind, I guessed—leaned against one wall. Ropes hung from the beams in the ceiling. Tangles of wooden blocks—they looked like they'd been made out of driftwood—dangled like bunches of bananas from another beam. Against the other wall were wooden buckets, rusty iron wheels, some more scrap iron and a little stack of what looked like carved bowls with lids on them. I picked one up and lifted the lid to look inside.

"It's an eating bowl," someone behind me said, startling me so badly that I dropped the bowl onto the packed earth floor. I spun around and saw Tryggvi in the doorway, bent over so that he could look inside. "I didn't intend to startle you," he said. "Einar asked me to drop by and pick up a few things for Sigurdur. They want to keep him in the hospital for a few days." He glanced around. "What are you doing in here?"

"Just looking around." My heart was just starting to slow to its normal pace. "So is he okay?"

"Sigurdur? I don't know." He bent and picked up the wooden bowl and lid that I had dropped. "This is from the old days," he said. "My afi—you know what that is, *afi*?"

"Grandfather," I said.

He seemed pleased. "My afi used to tell me stories about what it was like when he was young. He said they broke their backs farming all summer, and then they went to sea to fish all winter. If they were lucky, they made it back."

I thought about Gudrun's father, who had died at sea.

"He told me about these too." He turned the bowl around in his hands. "In the old days, people used these bowls instead of plates. Everyone would get a bowl of food in the morning. The lid was supposed to keep it warm during the cold winter days.

What was in the bowl was your ration. You ate it throughout the day, and when it was finished, that was it. You had to wait until the next day." He dropped the lid on top and handed it back to me. "People back in America would think they were starving to death if all they got was a bowl of food this size to eat every day, isn't that right?"

I supposed it was.

"And those there?" He pointed to the pieces of wood strung with rope and hanging in bunches from the rafter. "Those are loom weights. Back then, almost all the clothes were made from wool. Everyone had sheep. Everyone knitted. The women spun the sheep's wool to make yarn and thread. The men—like my afi—spun horsehair. It made good strong rope."

He looked around at the other stuff in the shed.

"Well, I'd better get going," he said. He ducked out of the shed and then stood in the doorway, waiting for me.

I peered around again. Maybe there was something in here that meant something to the old man, but I sure couldn't see what. I glanced at Tryggvi. He was waiting for me to emerge. I decided to come back later.

Just as we left the shed, a Lexus SUV pulled up beside what I assumed was Tryggvi's personal vehicle, and Karl got out. He was dressed in civilian clothes.

"Yo, boss!" he shouted.

Tryggvi glanced at him in annoyance.

"They said you were out here. A guy named Oli showed up at the station an hour ago," Karl said as he came toward us. "Says he has some information about that rash of tourist break-ins."

"Someone else will have to talk to him. It's my day off and I'm busy," Tryggvi said.

Karl shrugged. "Okay. But he says if you're not there in the next thirty minutes, he's walking and you can figure it out on your own. Now, I don't know about you, but all that negative publicity we got this summer sure didn't make the local merchants happy, to say nothing of the town council. And heaven knows what they're thinking of us in Reykjavik…"

Tryggvi's annoyance deepened into a scowl as he thought this over.

"I need you to run an errand for me then," he said brusquely. He told Karl what Sigurdur needed, and with another glance at me, he strode to his car and drove away. Karl continued on toward the house. I trotted after him, digging in my pocket for my key to the house. But he didn't need it. He tipped back a big rock near the front steps and pulled out a key to unlock the door.

"I'm going get the old man's things from his room," he said.

"No problem."

I flopped down on the couch in the living room to wait. Karl appeared ten minutes later with a small suitcase.

"Hey, I have an idea," he said. "Why don't we run into the city? I'll drop this stuff off for Einar and show you around. What do you say?"

"Actually, I was planning to hang around here, maybe do a little reading." I nodded at the book on the coffee table that I had begun and abandoned.

"Aw, come on," he said. "It's my day off. And I don't get to spend a lot of time with folks from back home."

"I'm from Canada," I reminded him.

"Same thing. Hey, have you tried the hot dogs here yet?"

"No, but—"

"You gotta try them. Icelandic hot dogs are famous. Bill Clinton loved them."

Yeah, well, Bill Clinton loved Big Macs too. And a lot of other things that weren't necessarily good for him or his career.

"Come on. I insist." He was grinning like a kid. "I'll take you to see the original geyser. And Gullfoss—the Golden Waterfall. My treat."

"Well—"

"You got plenty of time to read later. I need a break and for once I'd like to be able to talk to someone who understands ballpark franks, the Dodgers, the Knicks and the Giants—and by Giants I don't mean those crazy invisible people that lived under rocks either."

I said yes only because he kept pestering me the way I used to pester the Major when I was a little kid and didn't understand the concept of Immoveable Force.

We got in the Lexus suv.

"Nice ride," I said. "Cops must do okay over here."

"Nah," he said. "Everything over here is expensive. Apart from sheep and fish, they have to ship everything in. But after the big bust, there were a lot of people with cars they still owed money on, so I picked this baby up for a song. And I take good care of her. That's the Icelandic granddad in me. You take good care of your things and they'll take good care of you. Mind if I put on some music?"

I said I didn't and instantly regretted it. It turned out Karl was a major Rush fan. Talk about your golden oldies! Geddy Lee was older than my dad. But then the Rolling Stones were still rocking it out, and Mick and Keith were older than Grandma Mel.

Karl shouted over Geddy's shrieks all the way into Reykjavik, telling me about the old days in Iceland and the boom days and then the crash. From the way he talked, I guessed none of it had affected him. But that's the way it goes, right? Back home and in the States, the worse things get for regular people, the more prisons they build and the bigger and better armed the police get. Makes sense, right? You cut back recreation programs for kids, make sure the best they can hope for in life is to bag burgers or stand at registers cashing through cut-rate goods from China, and then you act all surprised when they take whatever cash they have, get zoned out of their heads and get themselves into trouble.

Gotta get tough on that youth crime. Gotta crack down on the little hooligans.

"What about kids here?" I asked.

"What about them?"

"You have a youth crime problem in Iceland?"

He laughed. "Everybody's got a youth crime problem. But what the kids get up to here isn't half as bad—heck, it's not even a quarter as bad—as what I used to see back in the Bronx."

I bet.

"You want to come up?" he asked when he finally pulled up in front of the hospital.

"Nah."

"Right," he said with a grin. "You're afraid Einar'll chew your head off for aiding and abetting, huh?" When I looked surprised, he said, "Brynja ratted you out." He got out of the car and swung the little suitcase out of the backseat. "Back in a flash."

It took longer than a flash.

And he didn't come back alone. Einar and Brynja were with him.

I braced myself.

It wasn't Einar who was angry. It was Brynja. And she was angry with me, which I didn't understand until Einar had shoveled her into the backseat and then stepped away from the car to have a chat with Karl.

"What are you doing here?" she hissed at me. "As soon as he knew you were here, he made me leave. I have to go with you and Karl and see the sights. I've already seen all the sights. I've seen them to death."

Gee, I really hated to be the one to break the news to her, but I said, "Karl would have showed up anyway. Your dad called your uncle and asked him to bring stuff for your grandfather. He had to go to work, so Karl's pinch-hitting for him." She frowned, and I had to explain what I meant. "Your dad probably would have got your uncle to drive you back. No offense, but he doesn't seem like a guy with a high tolerance for people disobeying his orders." And I should know. I lived with the Major.

The look she gave me said, *If it was legal, I'd kill you. Or at least punch you good and hard someplace good and sensitive.*

Karl got back behind the wheel.

"Okay," he said jovially. "Who wants a hot dog?"

Guess who did. And who didn't.

FOURTEEN

I'll say one thing for Karl—he loved his grandfather's country. After we hit the hot dog stand that Bill Clinton made famous, and had a pretty good hot dog, he took us to Hallgrims Church in the middle of Reykjavik, despite a lot of sighs of disgust and eye-rolling from Brynja. You can see the place from just about anywhere in the city. I'd been wondering what the heck it was. The place took forty years to build—and I'm not talking about medieval construction. It was started in 1945. And it's weird-looking, kind of like a volcano that's morphing into a spaceship. But it wasn't so much the church that Karl was pumped about. It was the view from the steeple. From nearly 250 feet above the ground you could see the whole of Reykjavik, and the ocean and countryside beyond—while you froze to death from the wind that whistled through the open windows.

From there we went to Thingvellir, where the original settlers met every year for the oldest contin-uously running parliament in the world. I was expecting some big spectacular buildings, but there were none. The old-timers met in summer and the whole thing was held outdoors. We also went to Geysir, where the word *geyser* comes from. Geysir, which he pronounced GAY-seer, used to shoot boiling hot water 30 feet in the air regularly for hundred and hundreds of years. It doesn't anymore. Talk about a letdown. But right near it there's another geyser that spouts every five minutes. It's actually pretty cool. As advertised, we also hit Gullfoss—Golden Waterfall. It's no Niagara Falls, but it's all right.

By the time we'd done all that, it was getting late. Karl drove Brynja and me back to the house. Einar's car was in the driveway, and he came to the door to greet us and to ask Karl if he wanted to stay for dinner. Karl said thanks but, believe it or not, he had a date. I don't know why that was supposed to be hard to believe—he was a nice enough guy and I guess he wasn't all that bad-looking.

Einar called us into the kitchen and got Brynja to set the table. He'd made chicken and rice with a side of canned peas. It was okay. Actually, since all I'd had to eat all day was a hot dog, it was better than okay. I polished off two helpings.

Einar leaned back in his chair and got down to business.

"I know we were supposed to leave tomorrow," he said. "But we won't have the test results until Monday."

Aw, man! I could see where this was going.

"It's okay," I said. "If you can just recommend someone else who can take me…"

"I was hoping you would wait so that I can do it. It would mean a lot to Sigurdur."

"I know but…I really appreciate everything you've done for me. It's been great. But I was kind of hoping to get this done sooner rather than later." Not to mention I didn't think I could handle four or five more days with Brynja. "I could even go by myself if you point me in the right direction." I figured in a country as treeless as this, how hard could it be?

No matter where you were, you could see for miles in any direction.

"It wouldn't be safe for you to go alone. The roads are bad, there's not much around and the weather is unpredictable. You need a guide and a proper vehicle. You also need to take precautions."

Really? He hadn't been out in the middle of absolutely nowhere with Worm. If I could survive that, I could survive anything.

"If I get another guide, it'll be one less thing for you to worry about."

"Let him go with someone else, Dad," Brynja said. "We need to look after Afi."

Einar nodded reluctantly. "I'll make some calls tomorrow," he said. "I'll let you know."

I was so grateful that I insisted on cleaning up the kitchen. I did a great job too. It would have passed any white-glove test the Major threw at me. I had just finished when my cell phone rang. It was Geir.

"I found something," he said, "but I don't know if it's what you were looking for."

I glanced at Brynja, who had stationed herself at her father's computer, and walked out of the room. The living room was empty, so I took the call there.

"There was a woman who was found frozen to death in the interior, near Askja."

Askja. That was near where I was supposed to take the journal.

"When?" I asked. I heard paper rustling.

"She was found in 1944."

1944? That was too late.

"But," Geir said, "she had been missing for two years."

"Since 1942. Does it say what happened?"

"No. Only that she was found. That was near where your grandfather's plane crashed, wasn't it?"

"Yes." It was also near where he had woken up and found Sigurdur taking care of him. It was where he had seen a red scarf that Sigurdur said he must have imagined.

"She may have been lost," Geir said, "although I can't imagine what she would have been doing out there in the first place. It seems more likely that she just decided to walk out into the storm…"

"What do you mean? Why would anyone do that?"

"I mean that she may have walked out with no intention of coming back."

Oh.

"Did you find out anything else?" I asked.

"Her name—Kerstin Torsdottir. Age twenty-three. She was reported missing by a friend in Reykjavik, where she was living at the time. The friend is deceased— I checked. But here's something. Before she moved to Reykjavik, she worked for a doctor near Borgarnes."

Near Borgarnes? Maybe he was still alive. Or…?

"Do you have his name?"

"Well, this is where it gets funny."

"Funny?"

"His name is Sigurdur."

"Sigurdur?"

"Gudrun's grandfather. I don't remember Gudrun ever mentioning Kerstin, but then I can't see why she would. It was all a long time before she was born."

Kerstin used to work for Sigurdur. Kerstin was out in the blizzard after my grandfather's plane crashed. Sigurdur denied any knowledge of her to my grandfather, but had had a strong reaction to the sketches in my grandfather's journal. Sigurdur had the weight of a secret on his mind, something that he had been about to show me, something that he had been trying to point out to me…

"I don't know if that helps you at all, Rennie." Geir said. "But it's all I could find."

"It's great, thanks," I said. "I really appreciate it."

"It was nothing." There was a pause. "But there is something *you* can do for *me*."

"Name it."

"When you asked me about Gudrun, it brought back a lot of memories. I went into storage and looked through her notebooks—the ones the police returned when they closed the case. I didn't delve into it then. I guess I didn't want to think about her ending her life like that. But I was wondering... you said you read French."

"My father is from Quebec—he's Francophone."

"If I get the pages to you that are in French, can you tell me what they say?"

"Probably."

We arranged that he would email scans of the pages to me. I promised to get back to him as soon as I could.

I dropped my phone back in my pocket, turned around—and got the start of a lifetime. Brynja was standing in the doorway, her arms crossed over her chest, staring at me.

"What were you saying about my afi?" she asked.

"Nothing. Jeez, do you always eavesdrop on people?"

"I wasn't eavesdropping. Just the opposite. I was trying *not* to eavesdrop."

"By standing there listening to me?"

"I was going to my room. I saw you were on the phone and I didn't want to disturb you, so I was waiting for you to finish."

"And while you waited, you listened in?"

"I heard you say my grandfather's name. Who were you talking to? What did they say about him?"

"Nothing. And anyway, it's none of your business."

"So you *were* talking about him?"

I did something then that surprised even me. Something I never in a million years thought I would do. I fixed her with the same steely look that I had seen in the Major's eyes a million times and I said the same words I had heard the Major say a million times and in the exact same tone of voice.

I said, "I'm not discussing this with you. It doesn't concern you."

It worked on her the same as it always worked on me.

She glowered at me. She opened her mouth to argue but then said, "Fine. I'm out of here," which is pretty much what I always said. The lines of communication had been broken. She yelled something to her father, who appeared almost instantly at the top of the stairs.

"When will you be back?" he said in English— I think for my benefit.

"Tomorrow evening. Johanna and I planned this ages ago, before you even knew *he* was coming." She shot another killer look my way.

Einar came downstairs and said something to her in Icelandic. She kissed his cheek, grabbed a massive purse that was stuffed almost to bursting and marched out of the house. A moment later I heard a car engine. Headlights streamed through the living-room window for a few seconds before arcing away.

"She's spending the night with some girlfriends," Einar said to me. "You don't mind?"

"Not at all," I said. Talk about an understatement!

"I've had a long day. I'll see you in the morning," he said.

"Sure. Is it okay if I read down here or watch some TV or something?"

"No problem. There's satellite."

He disappeared up the stairs.

I planned to watch TV until I got sleepy enough to turn in. At least, I'm pretty sure that's what I planned to do. But Geir's revelation kept turning over and over in my head. Why had Sigurdur seemed so uncomfortable when my grandfather asked him about the woman he had seen out in the interior? Why didn't Sigurdur want me to show the journal to Brynja and her father? What had he wanted to show me (or my grandfather) desperately enough that he'd dragged his tired and sick body out of bed to do it? What had he been pointing at? What was out there?

I watched half a movie—don't ask me what it was because I can't remember. My eyes were staring at the screen, but they weren't really *looking* at it. They were replaying the interior of that turf hut. There had to be something in there. It was the only thing he could have been pointing at.

I notched the volume down. There was no sound upstairs.

I waited another ten minutes. And another ten. Then another ten.

I left the TV on and tiptoed upstairs. The door to Einar's bedroom was closed, and there was no light showing under the door. I crept down to my room and pulled my nearly empty duffel bag out from under the bed. I felt around inside until I found what I was looking for and then I crept back out into the hall, pausing at the top of the stairs to take another look at Einar's door. It was still closed. There was still no light showing. I was pretty sure he was asleep.

But I waited another twenty minutes, just in case.

With the TV still on, I slipped on my jacket, tiptoed outside and closed the front door softly behind me. I didn't think Einar would get up. But if he did, if he had to use the bathroom or something, he would hear the TV and assume I was still watching it. I was betting he wouldn't check on me. He didn't seem the type.

I stumbled down the front steps. Being out here was like being out in ranch country. When it was dark, it was dark. There was no ambient light— no streetlights, no electronic billboards, no office lights left on in big office towers. Nothing.

Still, I waited until I was well away from the house before I turned on the small but powerful flashlight that the Major had insisted I pack, "just in case." I kept it pointed downward so I could see the way with an absolute minimum of light.

When I reached the turf hut, I held the flashlight between my teeth and I tugged on the door. I stepped inside and closed the door behind me. Then I began to search. There had to be something in here. I went to the eating bowls first and opened them one by one, looking for…well, I wasn't sure what I was looking for.

I searched behind the farm implements. I ran my fingers carefully over the beams. All I got for my trouble was a splinter. I stood in the middle of the little shed and shone my light over every inch of it, turning bit by bit until I had examined the whole beam-and-turf ceiling and every nook and cranny of the rough rocky walls.

Nothing.

This was ridiculous. Maybe I hadn't found anything because there was nothing to find. Maybe there was no secret either. The old man had called me David. He'd been delusional. Maybe whatever he wanted to show me was just that too—a delusion. I swung around to leave when my flashlight fell on something I hadn't noticed before. It was on the back wall of the hut, which was made of stone. From the outside, the hut looked like a long hill. When I'd first come in, I'd been surprised by how small it was and thought that maybe whoever had built the shed had dug only so far back into the hill. But my flashlight showed that there were tiny spaces between the rocks that made up the back of the hut. I had to duck down to get a closer look. I shone the flashlight through one of the little gaps. I was thinking it was probably just stones piled up in front of earth to make a strong wall.

But it wasn't.

I had no idea what was behind the rocks, but whatever it was, it's wasn't just dirt. I shone my light over the surface of all the rocks until I found a gap that was a little bigger than the others. I knelt down, put the head of the flashlight up close and pressed my face against the rock to try to see what was on the other side.

That was when I heard something behind me. A sort of swishing sound. It's also when I remembered the first time I had opened the wooden door to get into the shed.

Out of the corner of my eyes, I saw a man's boot. Einar.

I started to turn around. My mind clicked through possible explanations I could offer for what I was doing: I couldn't sleep, I have a keen interest in Icelandic history, I always wanted to examine the inside of a turf shed…No way. The truth looked like it was going to be my best option. Then the beam of my flashlight bounced off something on the other side of the wall. What *was* that? I was torn between wanting to take a second look and wanting to straighten up and start talking, fast.

The decision was made for me.

The last thing I remembered was something big and hard coming right at me—and making contact, I guess, because after that, it was lights-out.

FIFTEEN

I vaguely remember being picked up. I remember loud noise, like an engine. A helicopter engine? It's the only way I figure I could have woken up in the middle of nowhere.

Yeah, I definitely want to get even.

Also, I don't want to die, not like this, not out in the middle of nowhere.

I stumble through the snow until I'm exhausted. I have to rest, but I'm afraid that if I do, that will be the end of me.

My knees buckle.

I peer around. My eyes hurt, but I can't tell if that's because of the snow and the cold or if something happened to them when I was hit. I can't see any place to take shelter. Everywhere I look, all I see is snow. Endless stretches of it. It's like the North Pole out here, or, at least, what I imagine the North Pole looks like. The only things missing are polar bears and Inuit. Polar bears I can live without, but I'd be pretty glad to see an Inuit hunter right about now, someone who would know how to handle himself in a blizzard. He'd probably whip out a knife and start cutting snow blocks to make an igloo—assuming his grandfather had showed him how. Me? I don't have a clue.

Not a clue.

But maybe there is something I can do.

I pull the sleeves of my sweatshirt down over my hands and start digging in the snow. I keep going until I've made a nice deep hole. I crawl into it. The wind whistles over my head, but at least it isn't whistling all over me. I can't say I'm exactly warm because I'm not. Not even close. But at least I'm out of the wind. I huddle in that position, my arms wrapped around my knees, my head and chest down over my arms, making myself into the smallest people-sicle I can. Somehow, even though I know it's about the most dangerous thing I can do, I fall asleep.

I don't know how long I sleep. All I know is that the wind has died down when I wake up. It's still snowing, and my feet are numb. That scares me more than I've ever been scared in my life. What if they're frozen solid? What if I end up with frostbite? What if they have to cut my feet off? I try to wriggle my toes, but I can't tell if they're moving.

I feel sick deep inside and the feeling grows and mutates, like an alien pathogen, a feeling of terror, despair, hopelessness, a feeling like I want to cry, and then I do. I feel the tears sting my cheeks, probably giving them frostbite too. Where am I? How did I end up here? Why didn't I just keep my nose out of things? I've practically made a career out of that the past couple of years: telling people I don't care, acting like I really and truly don't care, not wanting to care because what's the point if it can all vanish, just like that. Like my mom. Like this.

I'm going to die.

I'm numb all over. I feel like my body doesn't exist anymore, it's just me and my brain sending waves of panic through me, telling me it's all over, I'm finished, I might as well just go back to sleep and let it happen. That's supposed to be the thing about freezing to death. It's supposed to be painless. You just lie down and go to sleep and never wake up again. Maybe I could dream about Mom. Maybe I could manage, for once, to picture her the way she used to be, the way she really was, not the way she ended up. That would be nice.

Do you really see your life flash before your eyes just before you die? If that turns out to be true, she'd be there. She'd be the biggest part of it. My mom and her smile. My mom and the flowery scent of her as she sat beside me at the kitchen table and patiently explained a math problem for the hundredth time. She was always patient. Always soft-spoken. She never yelled. She never said anything mean. She never made me feel stupid when I didn't understand something or like a failure when I messed up. She just wanted to understand—what happened and what can we do to make it better? And when she said *we*, she really meant it. How can I help you, Rennie? Not like teachers or principals or vice-principals who said *we* when they meant *you* and never let an opportunity to express their disappointment go by. So there we were in the car, me being a total pain, bugging her to take a side trip she didn't want to take so that I could buy some comics I didn't really need to impress a kid at school I didn't really like. I'd just wanted to show him up for once. I'd driven her crazy when all she wanted to do was get home to the Major, which I never understood; he was such a hard-ass.

And she'd caved.

I'd pumped the air, like I'd scored a game-winning touchdown.

The next thing I knew, we were driving down a twisting road blasted out of the Canadian Shield and seeing Danger: Falling Rock signs every 10 kilometers or so.

And then I'd seen something I'd never be able to forget.

Lie down, Rennie. Close your eyes. Imagine. Picture her. Remember how good it was. How good *she* was. Especially compared to the Major.

Mr. Two Choices.

That's all it ever comes down to with him: two choices. Black and white. Do or don't do.

Succeed or fail. He's like a military Yoda: "There is no try." Don't go crying back to him that you did your best. If you'd done your best, you would have passed that test, made that team, got that job. Do or don't do. Make your choice.

Lie down or stand up.

Stay where you are or keep moving.

Quit or keep on slogging.

And that's when that old revenge streak of mine kicks in again. I can either let whoever did this to me win, or I can make it out alive and kick their ass.

If I fail a math test, it's no big deal. Who cares about math?

But if I let some bully take me out on the way home—that's a different story. Nobody takes out Rennie Charbonneau, not without a fight.

Nobody's going to kill me either. Not without a fight.

Keep walking, kid. Keep on slogging.

I have no idea how long I keep going. My watch is gone. My phone is gone.

I have no idea what direction I'm going in.

I just keep moving one foot in front of the other until I'm ready to collapse. Then I hunker down in another snow pit and do my best to stay awake and angry. When I'm angry enough, I get up and walk some more.

Eventually it stops snowing.

I keep walking.

It starts to rain, and I shake all over.

I keep walking.

While I walk, I think about the old man and what he'd wanted to show me. I think about the turf shed and what I had seen—well, almost seen—back behind that stone wall. I think about Freyja and Baldur and Barnafoss. I think about the woman's face sketched in my grandfather's journal.

I keep moving, right foot, left foot, right foot, left foot—even when I feel weak-kneed and feverish. I cup my hands and drink some rainwater. I remember that a person can go longer than they think without food but that water is a necessity. I'm sure in the right place for water—surrounded by snow and ice, glaciers, rain, geysers, waterfalls. Water is the one thing the Icelanders are never going to run out of. And whatever else happens to me, I'm not going to die of thirst.

I trudge.

I rest.

I drink.

I trudge some more.

The shaking gets worse. My teeth chatter. My clothes are soaked clear through to my skin.

Then the clouds thin and it starts to get warmer. But I'm shaking uncontrollably. The word *hypothermia* pops into my head. If a person's body cools too much, it can cause death.

I wish the Major was here with me. He'd know what to do.

When was the last time I wished that?

How about never?

I picture his face when they finally give him the news. *We're sorry to inform you, Major Charbonneau, but your son is missing in Iceland and is presumed dead. We're sending out search parties, of course, but it's been a few days now and we're not hopeful…*

He'll be disappointed. That goes without saying. Maybe he'll even be upset. But there will also be a part of him that will say, *Well, I can't say that I'm surprised.*

If it was anyone else's son, yes. But my son? No, I'm not surprised at all.

My knees buckle. I fall to the ground and lie there, facedown, crying, blubbering like a baby, too tired to get up, too afraid. It's getting dark again. This time I don't care.

SIXTEEN

I raise my hand over my face to shield it from the glare. Is this what they mean when they say you see a light at the last moment? Is this the light I'm supposed to walk toward? Is it the light that will guide me to my mother?

I struggle to a sitting position and lower my hand, squinting into the brilliant sun. Everywhere is whiteness, the way I imagined heaven to be when I was a little kid. Except it isn't the white of clouds. It's the white of snow.

Mostly.

I stand up. The whiteness stops in the distance and becomes black. I see something move. It looks like...

I squint.

It is. It's a horse. All by itself.

Correction, all by itself with a couple of other horses.

I try to take a step and crumple to my hands and knees. I stay in that position, panting, until my hands begin to freeze. I force myself to get up again. I try again to take a step. My feet are so heavy that the best I can do is shuffle. I keep my eyes on those horses in the distance, tiny as raisins, and shuffle toward them. I don't remember thinking about anything. I don't remember feeling anything. I just stare at those sturdy little Icelandic horses and stumble toward them like my life depends on it.

Which it does.

At first, I'm giddy with excitement. Where there are horses, there are bound to be people. But no matter how many steps I take, the horses don't get any bigger. They stay tiny, so tiny that when I hold my thumb up to one, it completely disappears behind it.

It crosses my mind that I'm seeing things. The horses aren't really there. They're just figments of my imagination. Maybe I'm not even walking. Maybe I'm still lying in the snow somewhere, close to death, dreaming that I'm walking, the same way I'm dreaming that I see horses. I'm dreaming hope for myself, release from everything I've been through. But the release isn't going to be what I thought. I'm never going to get to those horses. They aren't going to lead me home. And home isn't what I imagined either. Home isn't going to be the Major. It's going to be Mom.

Then, so fast I hardly believe it, the horses get a little bigger.

My heart starts to hammer in my chest.

I can see the edge of the snow clearly now. The horses are just beyond it. They *are* getting bigger.

And bigger.

They keep their distance from me as I stagger toward them. The snow and ice slant downward. I trip and careen down an icy slope. Sounds like fun. Isn't. The ice is bumpy and jars every bone in my body.

Then the ice stops.

Just like that.

Stops at the edge of nothingness. But I'm still shooting forward.

I claw at the ground. I kick my feet straight out in front of me, trying to dig them in.

I feel myself lift off the ground, heading toward the nothingness—a huge abyss.

I think I scream.

My hands scrabble around for something to hold on to.

I feel myself falling, falling.

My fingers make contact with something. Grab at it.

My shoulders feel like they're being ripped from their sockets.

My feet kick out into nothingness.

I hold tight to…I crane my neck upward…I hold tight to a spike of ice. I try to ease my other hand up to grab it, praying the whole time that it won't snap off. I refuse to let myself look down and concentrate instead on getting a good grip and then swinging my feet to the side of the abyss to hunt for a foothold. Think about the task at hand, Rennie. Forget about everything else. Nothing else matters. Hold tight. Find someplace to put one foot.

My toe digs deep into a little hole.

My other foot dangles uselessly.

Then it catches too.

Now, slowly, ease yourself up. That's it. Push. You can do it. Forget how tired you are. Forget how sore you are. Push.

I push.

My head comes up above the top of the chasm. I dig in with my hands and push again to get one foot over the edge. I flop onto the snow at the top and pull up my other leg. I crawl away from the edge of the abyss.

Only then do I look down.

I freeze.

There is nothing down there.

Nothing as far as I can see.

I scramble back from the edge on my hands and knees. Then I crawl, still on my hands and knees, around the edge of the abyss. Only then do I stand. My legs shake. My hands shake. Jeez! I pick my way down the remainder of the slope. It takes forever, but now I know the truth of the old saying: "Haste makes waste." It almost made waste of me.

The sun is going down again by the time I'm off the snow—off, I think, the glacier.

I keep going. It isn't easy. There's no snow, but it's cold, especially as the sun sinks, and the terrain is uneven. I'm on volcanic rock now. A lot of it is covered with lichen, which makes it look pillowy soft, but I find out the first time I trip and thrust out a hand to steady myself that there's nothing soft about it. I cut my hand open—but I don't feel a thing. I'm numb, and that scares me more than anything else.

When it's too dark and I'm stumbling too much, I feel gingerly around for someplace to rest. I hunker down into a little ball again to preserve as much warmth as I can.

I wake to a sunnier, warmer day, haul myself to my feet and set off again. I keep an eye out overhead for an airplane or a helicopter that might be passing. I don't see one all day.

I don't see anything all day.

The sun sets again.

And I see a light in the distance.

A couple of lights.

They look like lights from the windows of a house.

I keep walking. I don't care how many times I fall or even that I feel something warm and sticky on my right knee. I keep going. Go toward the light, Rennie. Go toward the light.

SEVENTEEN

The house turns out to be directly across from a restaurant and right beside a couple of gas pumps in the absolute middle of nowhere. I'm not kidding. A man answers my hammering. He looks around for my car, probably wondering why he didn't hear it drive up. When he doesn't see one, he looks baffled. He says something I didn't understand.

"I don't speak Icelandic," I say.

His eyes widen.

"You're American."

Whatever. I feel like I'm going to collapse in a heap at his feet.

"I got lost," I tell him. "I—"

"Come in." He stands aside to let me pass.

His house is as neat as any I've seen in Iceland. It's cozy too. A woman comes out of a back room to see what's going on. There are a couple of young guys there too. They're taller than the man, but they look just like him.

I start to tell them what happened. A version of it, anyway—the "getting lost" part. They take me into the kitchen, sit me down and wrap me in blankets. I ask for water and get it. The woman makes tea and I wrap my hands around the mug and enjoy every second of the heat. She also brings me a plate of lamb stew. I wolf it down and immediately feel sick. Too much too fast, I guess. I tell them I'm fine. The man doesn't believe me on the last point. He questions me about how long I've been gone, and I figure out it's been four days. I sit there for a while, wrapped in blankets in the warmth of the house, and I start to nod off. By then I've lost track of time. I'm dimly aware of the man saying something. He is talking to one of his sons. Then he tells me to come with him.

He takes me upstairs to a bathroom. One of his sons appears with a bundle of clean clothes. The man wants me to shower. He says before I get dressed, he wants to look at me. He wants to make sure I'm okay.

I shower. I wrap myself in a towel. I let the guy look at me. At my feet in particular. He says everything checks out. He sounds surprised when he says it.

"I must call someone." The way he says it, it sounds like he can't decide who that someone should be.

"Um, where am I exactly?" I ask.

He tells me, but it means nothing to me.

"I'll show you," he says. "After you get dressed."

I put on his son's clothes—they fit pretty well—and go back downstairs. The man has a map spread out on the kitchen table. He points to where his house was.

I stare at the map. I'm at least a 160 kilometers from where I started. I think again about the noise I remember and decide it must have been a helicopter. Einar has a helicopter for his business. He flies it himself.

"How can I get to Reykholt?" I ask.

"Reykholt? You came from Reykholt?"

I nod. "Is there a bus or something?"

"I should call someone," the man says again. "You have parents here? Relatives?"

"No one who would miss me." For all I know, it's true. "I just need to get to Reykholt."

"Oli will drive you in the morning."

Oli is one of his sons.

I say I'd appreciate it.

The woman makes me some tea. Then she shows me where I can sleep. I burrow under the thick eiderdown on the bed and fall fast asleep.

It's late—nine thirty—by the time I get up. The woman is in the kitchen. She makes me a hearty breakfast with plenty of hot coffee. While I eat, I notice a computer in the next room.

"Can I use it?" I ask the man. "I'd like to email my dad back home."

The man is so happy that I want to contact someone that he practically drags me to the computer. I log into my email account—and see that I have a message from Geir. He says he's located five of the six notebooks that Gudrun kept about her big investigative piece on Baldur and the Russians. He has no idea what happened to the sixth. It's possible it was lost.

Either that or the police forgot to return it. He's also attached scans of pages that contain notations in French. I open the attachment.

I start to read through the twenty or so pages of the scan, but there's nothing helpful.

I glance at the man, who's watching me from the doorway to the kitchen.

I skim the last page.

Something catches my eye.

I read it more carefully.

"It is okay if I print one page?" I ask.

The man nods.

I print the page, read it again as I pull it from the printer, and then fold it and stuff it into my pocket. I log out of my email account and off the computer, making a note to thank Geir later.

The woman has washed and dried my clothes. They smell fresh and lemony. I go and change into them. When I get back to the kitchen, Oli is waiting for me. I thank the man and the woman and follow Oli to an suv. We take off.

Oli has the radio on and he's humming along to a rock station. I'm thinking about that last page of Geir's email. Part of me doesn't want to believe

223

what I read. If I'm interpreting it right, Brynja will be hurt—maybe badly.

When I see a sign that says we're 50 kilometers from Borgarnes, I tell Oli I need to make a phone call. He offers me his cell phone.

"I don't have the number," I say. "I need a phone book."

He pulls over at the next restaurant–gas station we come to. He goes inside. I see him speaking to a woman behind the counter who hands him something. He comes back to the car and hands it to me—a phone book. He gives me that and his cell phone and says he's going to get a coffee, do I want one? I tell him I'm fine, thanks. When he goes back inside, I look up the number for the Reykholt police. I punch it into the phone and when someone answers, I ask for the only person I can think of who will believe me and maybe help me. I ask for Karl.

"Karl here," says a voice with a familiar Yankee accent.

"It's Rennie."

"Rennie? Where are you, son?"

I tell him.

"How the devil did you get there?" he asks. "Tryggvi has a search party out around Askja looking for you. That's where Einar figured you went. He said you were impatient to get there and didn't want to wait for him."

I bet he did.

"He tried to kill me," I say.

"What? Who?" He couldn't have sounded more surprised if I'd just told him I'd just escaped from the clutches of a troll.

"Einar. He knows I was nowhere near Askja. And Karl?" I hesitate. "I think Tryggvi's in on it."

"Look, Rennie, I don't know—"

"The last I remember, I was in a turf shed at Einar's. Then I woke up a hundred and sixty kilometers away. Einar must have dumped me there with his helicopter—"

"Now hold on. I've known Einar for a lifetime of summers. He's a good man. And Tryggvi— he's a pain in the butt, but he's a cop. Cops don't do stuff like that."

Sure they do. But I don't want to get Karl's back up. I need him.

"If Einar's such a great guy, why did he try to kill me? Why did he dump me in the middle of nowhere to freeze to death?"

"I don't know that he did," Karl says.

"I do. He knows where Baldur is too." Unless I'm wrong about what I saw, Baldur didn't leave the country at all. Quite the opposite. He was up to his eyeballs—well, his eye sockets—in it. "Meet me and I'll show you."

There's a long pause, then: "Where are you? I'll come and get you."

"I'm on my way back to Reykholt. I can be there in fifteen minutes. Twenty at the most."

"Okay. Okay. How are you traveling?"

"I hitched a ride."

"You know where that gas station is, just before the cut-off to Einar's place?"

I do.

"About a kilometer before that, there's a lookout. Tourists stop there. Get your guy to drop you there. I'll meet you there."

"Bring a pick and shovel," I say.

I get out of the truck and go into the restaurant where I find Oli sipping coffee and flirting with the young woman behind the counter. I wave to him, and he reluctantly slides off his stool.

Oli drops me off at the side of the road and waves as he executes a U-turn and heads for home.

I cross the road to a sign that points to the lookout. I follow a twisting path down a slope that ends in a secluded patch of lichen-covered land with a magnificent view of a waterfall. The fall is spectacular—high, multi-leveled, all foam and crystal water against black rock under a bright blue cloud-studded sky. I can see why the place is a favorite for tourists, but there are none around. I pull out the page I printed and read it again. If this doesn't prove that Einar was involved, I don't know what will.

Karl shows up five minutes later.

"Here." I thrust the paper at him.

He squints at it. "What language is this?"

"French."

He hands the page back to me.

"My Icelandic is good. Spanish I can manage—street Spanish. But French?" He shakes his head. "Never had a call for it. What is that?"

"It's a page from Gudrun's notebook."

He raises an eyebrow. "I'd be remiss in my duty if I didn't ask where you got that."

"I got it from someone who worked with Gudrun at the paper. Apparently she wrote her notes in French when she didn't want anyone to see what she was up to. As far as I can tell, no one at the paper speaks French." I point to a sentence halfway down the page. "She says here that she has to confront E—she means Einar—with something she found out but that she's afraid how he will react. So worried that she wonders if she should go straight to the police instead."

Karl frowns. "What are you thinking, Rennie?"

"That Einar knew something. Why else would she use that word—*confront*?" That would explain why he hadn't wanted Gudrun digging into that story. "He was the only one besides Baldur who knew what she was working on, so either she told him or Baldur did. On another page, it mentions that she thinks Baldur had a partner here in Iceland, someone with inside information about police investigations. Sounds like a cop to me. Baldur and Tryggvi used to be friends—good friends. Gudrun must have found out that Tryggvi was in on it with Baldur.

She may have suspected that Einar knew something about it and was keeping quiet. She wasn't sure what to do—talk to Einar or go straight to the cops."

Karl's frown deepened.

"Let me get this straight," he says slowly. "You think that Tryggvi killed Gudrun and that Einar knew about it?"

"I'm not sure who killed Gudrun," I say. I'd been chewing over that one for a while. If she knew about the deal Baldur and Tryggvi had made with the Russians, and if she knew what was behind the Russians' willingness to invest in Baldur's resort, and if she was going to expose it all, bring it all down around their ears, sure, Tryggvi could have done it. Or Baldur. Or, for that matter, the Russians.

"And Baldur? What happened to him?" Karl asks.

"He's dead."

"I suppose Tryggvi killed him too." He thinks I'm crazy. I can tell by his voice.

"I'm not one-hundred-percent sure about that either," I say.

"That's a lot of *not sures*, son."

"Maybe Baldur panicked and Tryggvi killed him. Or maybe the Russians killed him. Or maybe it was Einar.

But I know where Baldur is, and Einar and Tryggvi both knew it. That's why they tried to kill me. And when I talked to Freyja—"

"You talked to Freyja?"

I nod. "Einar knows it too. He saw me come out of her place. She told me that Baldur's car was found down near the port and everyone figured he left the country. But that's not what happened." I tell him what the old man said about seeing something bad, and where the old man had pointed. It had nothing to do with Kerstin. "I think Sigurdur saw Tryggvi, and maybe Einar, hide Baldur's body."

Karl thinks over what I've said. He looks far from certain.

"Let's go," he says finally. "Show me."

EIGHTEEN

Karl radios back to the police station and speaks to someone there in Icelandic. Then we drive the short distance to Sigurdur's place. On the way, I ask about the old man.

"He's still in the hospital," Karl says. "But the doctors think he'll be able to go home soon. Brynja's been pretty much camping out there. Oh, and she thinks you're an idiot for going to Askja on your own."

"I already told you—I was nowhere near Askja."

Karl turns off the road and onto the lane leading to Sigurdur's place. As we cross the bridge, I see that Einar's car is gone. I'm glad.

Karl parks and we get out. He pops the trunk and grabs a pick, a shovel and a flashlight. We walk side by side to the turf hut. My heart is beating fast. Finally I'm going to get a good look at what's on the other side of that stone wall. I'm going to see if what I saw glinting in the beam from my flashlight really is what it looked like. I think about Freyja and Brynja. Once that wall is broken down, they're both going to find out things they don't want to know.

"Look." I point to the quarter-circle on the ground where the grass has been scraped away by the opening and closing of the door. "When I first saw this shed, Einar said no one ever went in it. But you can see that someone has gone in and out—a lot. And when I climbed up to that waterfall one day"—I nod to the fall behind the house—"I saw Einar over here. He's got a guilty conscience, just like that guy in the Poe story."

"Poe?"

"Edgar Allan Poe. We read one of his stories in school. *The Tell-Tale Heart*. It's about a guy who kills someone and then goes crazy with guilt. I think Einar keeps checking the place, you know, to make sure no one has found out. Tryggvi must have told him he found me inside. Einar probably watched me after that and saw me go in again that night. Next thing I know, I'm in the middle of nowhere."

Karl looks doubtful. I guess I can't blame him. He knows Einar. He works with Tryggvi, and even if the two of them aren't best buddies, they're cops. Cops have it beaten into their heads that they have to stick together. He continues to look doubtful right up to the moment when I show him where to point his flashlight. He hunkers down and stares between the tiny gaps in the stone wall.

"You see it?" I say. "It's under that pile of rocks, but you see it, right?" It was a watch—I was sure of it—peeking out from under a man-sized pile of rock in what I was willing to bet was originally part of this turf hut, which explained why the hut looked smaller from the inside than it did from the outside.

Karl straightens up slowly.

"Well, I think you're on to something." He turns off the flashlight. "This fellow who gave you those notes in French, how come he didn't tell the police what was in them?"

"He didn't know. He doesn't read French, and I guess he didn't think they were important, not after

Tryggvi returned the notebooks. When he heard I read French, he asked me to take a look at them and tell him what they said."

"Did you?"

"Not yet. I haven't had a chance."

A shadow falls across the sunlight streaming in through the turf shed's door; then the light is blotted out as someone steps inside.

Einar.

"What's going on?" he demands. His eyes flick to me. He doesn't look surprised to see me.

"This boy was just showing me something interesting behind that wall, Einar," Karl says.

Einar looks at the wall and then back at me. "I don't understand."

"There's something back there," Karl says. "We need to break down the wall."

Einar stands motionless in the doorway. Any minute now he's going to turn and run, and Karl, like all Icelandic police, isn't wearing a gun.

"Well, Einar?" Karl says. "What do you have to say about this?"

"What do you want me to say?" Einar's voice is as dull as his eyes.

"It's Baldur, isn't it?" I say. "Did you kill him? Or was it—?"

"Hold on there, Rennie," Karl says. "Suppose you leave the questions to me."

No way. Not after everything I've been through.

"He tried to kill me," I say. "I deserve to know. Hell, if it wasn't for me, *you* wouldn't know. You wouldn't be here."

Karl heaves another sigh.

"That's true," he allows. He turns to Einar. "Well?"

Einar looks down at the packed-earth floor for a few seconds, like a kid staring at the toes of his sneakers after having been caught cheating on a test. And then he meets my eyes. I don't know the man well. But I know shame when I see it. Regret too.

"It was an accident," Einar says. "Baldur killed my Gudrun. I know he did. But there wasn't any proof—nothing the cops could use. He was going to get away with it. So I went to him. I tried to get him to do the right thing, to tell what he did. But he refused. And then—" He breaks off and draws in a few deep breaths to steady himself. "I just wanted him to do the right thing. I tried to make him go to the police.

235

But he fought me. What could I do? I fought back. I didn't mean to kill him. It was an accident."

I almost believe him about the accident part.

Almost.

"If that's true," I say, "if it was an accident, why didn't you tell the police what happened?" I'm on a roll. I know it. He's confessed to killing Baldur. Now I want him to tell the rest. I want him to spill whatever he knows, right here, right now—what he knew, what Tryggvi knew, what Gudrun knew.

"They would never believe me. Everyone knew I suspected Baldur. Everyone heard me call him a murderer. I would go to prison, and then what would happen to Brynja?" He gets a faraway look in his eyes, like he's staring into the past, reliving what he's done. "I should never have let Gudrun take that job. I don't understand why she wanted it. If she had stayed home, if she had never got it into her head to be a reporter, none of this would have happened. She would never have found out what Baldur did. He never would have killed her, and I never would have done what I did."

"Does Brynja know what you did?" I ask.

It takes a few seconds before Einar's eyes meet mine. He shakes his head.

Karl tosses him the pick. He's going to make Einar break down the wall. He going to make Einar expose what has lain hidden for the past year.

I'm watching him holding that pick. I'm wondering how he's going to explain this to Brynja. I'm wondering, too, how she will react.

Then I say, "How did you know?" because all of a sudden it's bothering me.

Einar doesn't even look at me.

"You said you knew that Baldur killed Gudrun," I say. "How did you know? Did she tell you she was going to meet him that night?" I pull the sheet of paper from my pocket. "She says here she's afraid of how you're going to react when she tells you something. She can't decide whether to confront you or go straight to the police. Did she tell you where she was going, is that it? Did she tell you what she suspected and what she was going to do, and you let her go? You let her meet Baldur and that's why you're so sure he killed her?" That had to be it. "You feel guilty," I say as the thought occurs to me. "You could have stopped her. You could have made her stay home that night. But you didn't."

"She didn't tell me anything," Einar says in a hushed voice. "She said she had to go out. She was acting strange. Quiet. She left and she never came back. Baldur killed her."

"But if you don't know where she went…" My voice trails off.

I think.

I remember what Geir told me: there were originally six notebooks, but he could find only five. He said that one of them must have been misplaced when it was returned—either that or the police had neglected to return it. But there's a third possibility, namely that Tryggvi destroyed one of the notebooks because it contained information that linked him to Baldur. Once the death investigation was closed, who would bother to look any further? No one had—until I turned up and started asking questions.

"How do you know Baldur killed her? How do you know Tryggvi didn't do it?" I say.

It would be easy for a Quantico graduate like Tryggvi to get rid of evidence that a murder had been committed. It would be just as easy for him to commit a murder and cover up whatever evidence there might be.

My head is spinning. Things fall into place.

Gudrun suspects Tryggvi's involvement. She tries to decide whether to talk to Einar first or the cops, but maybe doesn't do either. Maybe she goes straight to Tryggvi and presents him with evidence that proves he's involved with Baldur. I can see how that might go. She calls Tryggvi—or maybe he knows from Baldur that she's getting close and he calls her. They arrange to meet. Tryggvi tells her where. She goes. He hears her out. He realizes he's cornered. He has no choice—he kills her and makes sure there's no evidence left behind. That explains the outcome of the autopsy—undetermined.

But now Tryggvi has a loose end—Baldur. What if Baldur found out what he'd done? Or what if he even suspected it? He probably hadn't counted on murder being part of the deal when he borrowed money from the Russians. So Tryggvi whispers in his brother-in-law's ear, "Gudrun was investigating Baldur, so he killed her. But there's no evidence. We'll never be able to prove it." Einar goes to Baldur. Baldur denies killing Gudrun. He refuses to go to the police—

why would he? They fight; Baldur ends up dead. And Tryggvi—lucky Tryggvi—tells his brother-in-law that they have to hide the body so that Einar won't be arrested for murder. Ta-dah!

"Tryggvi?" Einar says. Why would Tryggvi hurt Gudrun?" I see confusion on his face, and it throws me.

"Tryggvi helped you hide Baldur's body, right?" I say. "He's the one who told you Baldur killed Gudrun, isn't he?"

"The boy knows what you did, Einar," Karl says. "Now everyone is going to know. Brynja is going to know." He nods at the pick in Einar's hand. "You know what you have to do."

Einar looks at the pick like he can't figure out how it got there. He shakes his head. Doesn't he get it? Refusing to knock down the wall isn't going to change a thing. It's going to come down with or without him.

"What would Anders think if he knew what his grandson had become?" he says.

Anders?

The two men stare hard at each other.

"Who is Anders?" I say.

Something Geir told me hits me like a sledge-hammer: the name of the cop who ran the death investigation on Gudrun.

"What's Tryggvi's father's name?" I ask.

At first I don't think anyone is going to answer. But finally Einar says, "Jens."

So that makes him Tryggvi Jensson. The cop who ran the investigation—the cop who was trained in the States—was Andersson, not Jensson.

There's only one other cop around here who was trained in the States. I turn to Karl.

"Anders is *your* grandfather," I say. According to Geir, Icelanders who emigrate have to adapt, and one of the things they have to adapt to is names frozen at a point in time. Karl's father, born here, would have taken Andersson as his surname when he moved to the States. Karl was born in the States, where he would have taken the same surname as his father. His name is Andersson too.

Karl is focused on Einar. "Do you want to go to prison, Einar? Because that's what's going to happen unless you do something."

Einar doesn't answer.

I start to move away, but Karl grabs my arms and wrenches me back.

"You have no choice, Einar," he says. "You tried to get rid of Rennie once and failed. You can't fail again."

Einar looks at Karl with dull eyes.

"We haven't got all day," Karl says.

"You said he would never survive out there," Einar says. "You said the problem was solved."

You said. He means Karl. I try to wrench free, but Karl has a viselike grip on my arm.

"You killed Gudrun, didn't you?" I say to Karl.

Karl doesn't look at me. "Better to get it over with, Einar," he says.

"Gudrun went to meet you," I say. I stare at his face. I can't read a thing. In the shadows, it's as gray and flat as a blank screen, and it tells me everything I need to know. "You killed her and you told Einar that Baldur did it. He knew that Gudrun was investigating Baldur, but he didn't know about you."

Karl ignores me. "If he gets away, I won't be able to protect you this time," he says to Einar.

"You were protecting yourself," I say. "She knew, didn't she, Karl? What did you tell her when you arranged to meet with her? Did you feed her a line?

Did you tell her you could explain everything?" I could just see it. "Did you tell her you were investigating yourself, but that it was all hush-hush until you made your case?"

Still nothing.

"She was afraid of how Einar would react because you two were friends when you were kids. Gudrun was afraid Einar would be disappointed in you—or maybe angry at her for what she turned up about you. So either she forced you to meet her or you lured her to the falls. Either way, the result was the same. You killed her."

Einar is staring at Karl now.

"Karl?" Einar's voice is quivering with emotion. "What is he talking about?"

"You tricked Einar into doing some of your dirty work for you. You made sure he dealt with Baldur, and then you told him to hide the body. That way he wouldn't push to find out more. He already had it settled in his mind. And it gave you something to hold over him—you could threaten to expose him if you had to. Just like you're doing now."

"Karl? Is this true?"

"Of course not," Karl says.

"Sigurdur saw you," I say to Einar. "Just before he collapsed, he wanted to show me something. He pointed to this hut. He saw you bring Baldur back here. He saw you drag his body into the hut. But he didn't say anything because he believed that Baldur had killed Gudrun—because you told him that's what happened, because that's what Karl told you." I turn to Karl. "And you destroyed the sixth notebook too."

"What notebook?" Einar says.

"Gudrun had six notebooks," I say. "They were all turned over to the police, but only five were returned. No one noticed until now. Karl destroyed the sixth one. I bet there was something in it that implicated him."

Einar is staring at his old friend now. "You did this? You killed Gudrun?"

"No," Karl says.

"Yes," I say. "It wasn't Baldur. It was Karl."

Karl surprises the daylights out of me when he reaches behind himself and pulls out a gun from under his jacket.

"I thought handguns were illegal in Iceland," I say.

Karl smiles. "Where there's a will, there's a way. Give me the pick, Einar."

"What are you going to do?" I say. "Kill me and then kill him and say you got here too late to save him?"

"If you can't take care of it, I will, Einar," Karl says.

"So it is true," Einar says.

"Don't be ridiculous. Give me the pick, Einar."

"Ask him where he was the night Gudrun died," I say to Einar.

Einar looks at Karl for an answer.

"I was at home," Karl says. "For god's sake, Einar!"

"I bet he wasn't at home. I bet he was meeting Gudrun."

"Give me the pick, Einar."

"He did it, Einar. He killed Gudrun."

Karl points his gun at me. "I've had about enough of you." He's going to shoot. I see it in his eyes.

Einar raises the pick again. His eyes are hard on Karl.

Karl swings the gun and fires at Einar. I see a dot of red on Einar's chest. It grows. Einar looks down at it, puzzled. He sinks to his knees and then crumples face-first into the dirt.

I reach up and grab one of the ropes hanging from a rafter. I swing it, and the pieces of wood strung to it catch Karl across the face. He staggers backward, still clutching the gun. I swing again, harder this time. The rope catches him and wraps around his throat. He drops the gun and claws at the rope to loosen it.

I dive for the gun. I'm on my feet pointing it at Karl at about the time he manages to loosen the rope. He's gasping for breath. He eyes the gun in my hand.

"You gonna shoot me, Rennie?" he says.

"Get down on your knees or you're going to find out."

He won't go down. Instead, he takes a step toward me, his hand outstretched.

"Give me the gun, Rennie, before someone gets hurt."

"Someone already got hurt." I nod at Einar. "Stay where you are or I swear I'll shoot."

He smiles and takes another step toward me.

A car door slams, and I hear Brynja call in Icelandic for her father.

"Brynja, call the police in Reykjavik," I shout. "Call the police in Reykjavik."

Karl lunges at me and takes me down in a tackle. I almost pass out from the impact. I hold the gun over my head, as far from him as I can, but he's on top of me, head-butting me before reaching again for the gun. I see stars. But I don't let go. I hit him as hard as I can with the gun butt. He collapses on top of me.

A shadow appears in the doorway. Brynja. She falls to her knees beside her father.

"Call the police, Brynja," I say. "And get an ambulance."

NINETEEN

After that, everything happens both fast and slow.

Brynja calls Tryggvi. Tryggvi calls the police in Reykjavik. It takes a while for them to sort everything out. In the meantime, Einar and Karl are loaded into ambulances. Brynja rides to the hospital with her father. A cop rides with Karl. After quizzing me, the remaining cops start to take the back wall of the turf hut apart. After they find the body, they take me in for questioning. It's hours before I hear that Einar is going to be okay. Even better, he comes clean about everything that's happened and says that it was Karl's idea to get rid of me. Karl is charged with two counts of attempted murder. That will hold him until the cops figure out his part in the deaths of Gudrun and Baldur. I also hear that they're going to take a hard look at his finances, including any off-shore accounts he might have. They let me go. I call the Major and fill him in on what has happened. To my astonishment, he stays calm. He doesn't yell at me. He talks to the cops and has me put up at a guesthouse in Reykjavik. He says he's taking the next flight to Iceland.

Two days later, the police say I can go home with the Major. There's just one problem. I have unfinished business.

I get the Major to drive me to the hospital. Just as I suspect, I find Brynja there, shuttling between her father and Sigurdur. On the way over, I was afraid she'd be angry to see me, but she isn't. Mostly she looks tired.

"Afi has been asking for you," she says.

"And I want to see him. But first I wanted to talk to you. Are you okay?"

She draws in a deep breath. Maybe I'm wrong, but it looks to me like she's fighting back tears.

"My father made a mistake," she says quietly. "A terrible mistake."

"Karl set him up. He used your dad to solve his own problems."

"I know." She holds herself up tall. "I'm going to live with my aunt until—until everything is sorted out."

Einar's sure to end up in prison. Even if he didn't mean to kill Baldur, he hid the body. It could be a hard sell to a judge and jury that it was an accident. He tried to kill me too, so I wouldn't be able to tell anyone what I found out in that turf hut. I wonder how long they'll keep him locked up—and what prisons are like in Iceland.

"I want to show you something." I pull my grandfather's journal out of my pocket and hand it to her. She stares at it and then at me. She opens it and pages through it. When she looks at me again, she's frowning.

"Who is this?"

"Do you recognize her?" I ask.

"She looks a lot like my grandmother." She's still frowning. "Where did you get this?"

I tell her everything I know about the journal and the woman whose face fills its pages. I show her the letter, but she has as hard a time reading it as I did.

"I don't understand," she says. "Why didn't Afi want me to see this?"

"I don't know."

She peers at me and finally nods.

"Come on," she says.

Sigurdur is propped up in bed. He looks better—even better than when I first arrived.

"I'm glad you're all right," he says.

"And I'm sorry about Einar—and about everything."

"It is a good thing," Sigurdur says. "The burden was getting heavier and heavier for Einar. And for me. It is good that there are no more secrets."

Brynja and I exchange glances. She hands the journal and the letter to Sigurdur.

"There still are some, Afi," she says.

And so the old man begins to talk. He's the oldest person I've ever met, and the story he tells is seventy years old, but his voice trembles as he tells it and tears fill his eyes. What it comes down to is he loved her. He loved Kerstin and, if you ask me, he never got over loving her. She worked for him when he was starting out as a young doctor. She kept his house and helped with his patients. He was going to ask her to marry him. But she fell in love with someone else—an air force pilot. She moved to Reykjavik to be closer to the base at Keflavik. She got pregnant. Her pilot boyfriend was sent on a mission, and the next thing she heard, he was missing and presumed dead. She went to the only place she knew to have her baby— back to Sigurdur. He looked after her. He delivered her baby. Then she heard from her boyfriend's parents. They wanted the child. They were adamant their granddaughter was not going to be raised in a place as backward at Iceland.

"They were very well off and extremely well connected. And they were American. She was terrified the government was going to let them have the child." So they cooked up a scheme—Kerstin and Sigurdur. They were going to say the child had died. Sigurdur was prepared to fake a death certificate.

"I thought if I did…" But his voice breaks off and tears spring to his eyes. Brynja squeezes his hand and says something softly in Icelandic.

Then Kerstin got a message, forwarded to her from Reykjavik. Her boyfriend wasn't dead after all.

He was on his way back to Iceland. They would be reunited soon. Everything would be fine.

Or it would have been if the plane, the one my grandfather was flying, hadn't got caught in that blizzard and crash-landed—and if Kerstin's boyfriend hadn't died in my grandfather's arms.

The air force knew where it had lost track of the plane. Searchers were ready to go out as soon as the blizzard cleared. Kerstin was determined to go with them. But every minute that she waited put her more on edge. What had happened to the plane? Had it landed—or crashed? If it had crashed, was he alive? Hurt? Unable to move? Maybe freezing to death while the searchers were waiting?

She knew the terrain—or thought she did. She set out to find the father of her child.

She found my grandfather instead. After she made sure he was safe, she pressed on. She never made it back.

"But why did you lie to my grandfather?" I asked. "Why did you tell him there was no woman?"

"David was a friend of the baby's father. The baby was at my house. I was afraid he would say something to the parents. Kerstin didn't want her baby raised by strangers in America. She wanted her raised here

253

among her own people. And"—he clutched Brynja's hand tightly—"it was *her* baby. So I signed the death certificate and sent it to the baby's American grandparents."

"The baby?" Brynja asked.

"Your grandmother. A beautiful child. She looked so much like her mother."

Brynja looks down at the floor. "So you're not really my afi?" she says finally.

A few seconds pass before her eyes meet Sigurdur's.

"What I did was wrong," he says. "But I raised your grandmother, and when she died, I raised your mother. If you're angry with me, I understand."

"I'm only angry that you didn't tell me. Or Mother. Or anyone."

"She—Kerstin—she wanted the baby to stay here. She didn't want it to go to America."

"I love you, Afi," Brynja says. "No matter what. But you should have told me. Then you wouldn't have had to carry such a burden yourself. I'm glad you kept the baby. I'm glad you're my afi."

A tear trickles down the old man's face as Brynja leans in and kisses his cheek.

Brynja turns to me.

"Are you still planning to take the journal out there?"

I glance at the old man, who says, "He should do what David wanted."

I look at his gnarled fingers clutching the journal. "I think if he had known the whole story, he would have wanted you to have it," I say. "To remember her by."

When I finally leave the room, Brynja follows me.

"Thank you," she says. "Thank you for being so kind to him."

I tell her it's nothing, and it's true. It feels good to do something nice for the old man. He deserves it.

Two days later, the Major and I are in the airport at Keflavik, waiting to board a plane home. I notice he keeps staring at me.

"What?" I say finally, looking up from the magazine I've been reading.

"You handled yourself well, Rennie," the Major says. "Your mother would have been proud of you. I know I am."

I almost fall off my chair. The Major proud of me? I guess there really is a first time for everything.

"And I'm surprised you let me come here in the first place," I say—which reminds me. "What did Grandfather say in that letter that Mr. Devine gave you?"

"That there was something you want to tell me but that you're afraid to."

It's true. I talked to Grandfather about it—about how I wanted to tell the whole story.

"He said that you're afraid of me," the Major says. "Are you?"

"Well, yeah. I mean, sometimes. You can be one scary dude."

"Your mother was never afraid."

"She's not like me. She was tough."

He smiles. "She was that. So are you. You're a lot like her." He stares out at the tarmac for a moment. "So, is there something you want to tell me?"

I have a feeling it's now or never.

"It's about Mom."

He nods.

"It's about what happened to her."

"*Je t'aime, mon fils*," he said. "*N'aie pas peur.*"

256

Don't be afraid. And at that exact moment, sitting on a molded plastic chair beside him at the airport, I'm not. I start talking, *really* talking, to the Major—my dad—for the first time in a long time. It feels good.

ACKNOWLEDGMENTS

A great big thank-you is owed to Eric Walters, who thought up the whole series and wrote the first book; to Andrew Wooldridge, who said yes; to Sarah Harvey, who kept track of all the fictional characters, all the authors, all the timelines and all the details; and to Shane Peacock, John Wilson, Ted Staunton, Sigmund Brouwer and Richard Scrimger, who wrote the other books in this series.

NORAH McCLINTOCK is a five-time winner of the Crime Writers of Canada's Arthur Ellis Award for Best Juvenile Crime Novel. Norah grew up in Montreal, Quebec, and now lives with her family in Toronto, Ontario. Visit www.web.net/~nmbooks for more information about Norah.

SEVEN
THE SERIES

7 GRANDSONS
7 JOURNEYS
7 AUTHORS
1 AMAZING SERIES

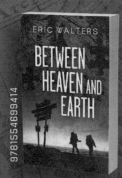